STO

FRIENDS
OF ACPL

3 1833 00808 32

D1159914

I Will Make You Disappear

Also by Carol Beach York

Christmas Dolls
Dead Man's Cat
Good Charlotte
The Midnight Ghost
Miss Know It All Returns
Mystery at Dark Wood
Mystery of the Diamond Cat
The Mystery of the Spider Doll
Nothing Ever Happens Here
One Summer
Sparrow Lake
Takers and Returners: A Novel of Suspense
Ten O'Clock Club
The Tree House Mystery
Where Love Begins

I Will Make You Disappear

by
Carol Beach York

THOMAS NELSON INC.
NASHVILLE / NEW YORK

No character in this story is intended to represent any actual person; all the incidents of the story are entirely fictional in nature.

Copyright © 1974 by Carol Beach York

All rights reserved under International and Pan-American Conventions. Published in Nashville, Tennessee, by Thomas Nelson Inc., and simultaneously in Don Mills, Ontario, by Thomas Nelson & Sons (Canada) Limited. Manufactured in the United States of America.

First edition

York, Carol Beach.
    I will make you disappear.

SUMMARY: Two young girls, spending a vacation with their family in a gloomy house, begin to play at witchcraft.
        [1. Witchcraft—Fiction]   I. Title.
PZ7.Y82Iaw   [Fic]   74-10272
ISBN 0-8407-6410-3

U.S. 1828312

For Gloria R. Mosesson—

friend and editor

I Will Make You Disappear

CHAPTER ONE

The house was shaded by a thick grove of trees. Not much sunlight reached the small rooms within. An air of shadowy gloom seeped from the corners and made the children shiver.

"I'm sure it will be better on sunnier days," their mother said. She went around raising window shades and trying to sound cheerful to hide her own surprise at the small, dim rooms. "Think how cool it will be with all the trees."

But the children were not much reassured. Dark-eyed Clara and thin Louise exchanged uneasy glances. The house was not what they had imagined a summer cottage would be like at all. Little Polly and Teddy looked up the stairway to where the bedrooms were. There were shadows on the stairs and dark places they did not want to pass through.

9

"Come up and bring the suitcases," Mrs. Astin said briskly. "Let's see what the bedrooms are like."

From the upstairs windows there was little to see except the branches of trees growing close around the house. As if they were trying to squeeze it to death, Louise thought.

The bedroom that Mrs. Astin said Clara and Louise could share had in it an old-fashioned bureau, a bedside table, and a rocking chair. The room's only ornament was a small black clock on the bedside table, but when Clara picked up the clock and tried to wind it, the stem would not turn. She shook the clock and held it to her ear to hear if it was ticking.

"You'll break it," Louise warned.

But Clara thought the clock was already broken, probably by the last family that had rented the house. In disappointment, she set it back on the table, its hands still pointing motionlessly to twelve.

Louise tried the bed and wondered if she would be able to fall asleep in this small dark house with the trees squeezing in upon her.

Last summer they had gone to Ohio to visit Aunt Esther's family. That had been a lot more fun, Louise thought. Aunt Esther's house had been big and sunny. A carnival had come to town, and Louise had won a pink stuffed elephant. On the Fourth of July they had all gone to the fireworks display. It was the most exciting vacation Louise could remember. She had written about it afterward at school: "What I Did on My Summer Vacation."

What would she have to write about *this* summer's vacation?

"Better start hanging up your clothes, girls." Their mother appeared momentarily at the doorway. Then her voice dwindled as she turned and went into another room, herding Teddy before her. "Polly and Teddy can have this bedroom across the hall. . . ."

Polly lingered behind with Clara and Louise and the clock pointing to midnight. "I don't like this house," she said. From her small rosy face two mournful eyes stared up into Clara's. Her mouth drooped.

Polly was going to cry, Clara thought, and she snapped open a suitcase with a reassuring gesture and began to lay her pajamas and blouses on the bed. "For heaven's sake, Polly. There's nothing wrong with this house. The furniture's kind of old, that's all."

"It's spooky."

"Don't be silly," Clara scolded. She pretended to be very busy unpacking the suitcase.

"Do you like it?" Polly stood so close that her little face touched Clara's arm.

"We'll only be here two months," Clara said, which was not really an answer.

Two months. It sounded like forever to Polly.

"Mama's calling you." Clara kissed the rosy face with the mournful eyes.

But when Polly was gone, there was still Louise

perched on the bed, hugging her knees and twisting a strand of limp hair. "I don't like this house either. I wish we could go to Aunt Esther's again."

"Help me put these things in the bureau," Clara said. "Do you want the top drawers or the bottom ones?"

Louise looked at the bureau, twisting her hair. Two months sounded like forever to her, too.

In the room across the hall Mrs. Astin was helping Teddy unpack. She was sure that if she didn't help him everything would get into the wrong place.

"Teddy," she said with exasperation, "you can look out the windows later. Come and help me unpack."

Why did she feel so cross? she wondered. There was no reason. They had rented a quiet tree-shaded house in the country for two lovely summer months. Everyone should be happy.

"Teddy, come away from the window. . . . Where are you, Polly?" Mrs. Astin raised her voice to call across the hall.

Teddy pressed his nose tighter against the window-pane. "There's a man out there."

"There is?" Mrs. Astin came to look.

In the driveway at the side of the house a battered blue Ford had pulled in behind Mrs. Astin's car. A man dressed in work clothes stood beside the car. His back was to the house, and Mrs. Astin could not see his face.

"Oh," she said suddenly, "that must be Joe Hooker. Mr. Parker at the real estate office said there was a

12

handyman who took care of this place. I'll have to go down and speak to him."

She turned from the window in time to see Polly hauling out things from the suitcases.

"Oh, not that way, dear . . . " Mrs. Astin hastened to the rescue as clothes tumbled to the floor. Polly was dragging out a doll from amid the socks and underwear, and a box of plastic farm animals turned upside down, spilling out tiny cows and pigs and chickens.

Mrs. Astin sighed. "Teddy, stop looking out the window. . . . I don't know why you children had to bring so many toys. . . . Polly, you're stepping on the handkerchiefs. . . ."

The man below turned, and Teddy saw his face. It was an old face, sun-darkened and seamed with lines, and the man looked up—right into Teddy's eyes, as though he had felt Teddy up there at the window watching him.

Teddy stared back for a moment with surprise, and then let the curtain drop back into place to hide himself from the man.

CHAPTER TWO

As the first days passed, Mrs. Astin and the children explored the woods around the house and took picnic lunches down to the stream that trickled nearby.

They drove into town to the swimming pool, and explored for ice-cream shops.

Sometimes they had dinner in town, for Mrs. Astin considered part of her vacation was not having to cook every meal at home. Polly and Teddy's favorite place was a hamburger stand, but Clara liked the Village Inn best. There were red candles on the red-checkered tablecloths, and a great bear's head was mounted on one wall. Louise didn't like *that* much. It made her skin prickly to look up at that head.

Mrs. Astin enjoyed anyplace that meant there were no dishes to do afterward.

At night they slept in the narrow little bedrooms with the tree branches pressing close to their windows. Sometimes when she lay in bed at night Clara thought she heard noises in the house, like ghosts walking on the old floorboards of the stairs. She would lie awake long after Louise, breathing softly beside her, was asleep. Occasionally a tree branch would scratch against the window, and one night just as Clara was almost asleep the black clock on the table began to tick.

Tick tick tick tick tick.

The sound came faintly and steadily in the darkness.

Tick tick tick tick tick.

Softly. Steadily.

And then, as suddenly as it had begun, the ticking stopped.

In the morning the hands of the clock were still at twelve.

"You probably dreamed it, Clara," her mother said, when Clara told her the next morning at breakfast.

"Maybe it's a magic clock that only ticks at night," Teddy said eagerly, peering at Clara over the rim of his glass of milk.

Clara stayed awake as long as she could the next night, listening in the darkness. But the clock was silent.

Joe Hooker, the handyman, came out to the house every day. He hung the front-porch swing, mowed the grass, mended a loose railing on the back steps—things Mrs. Astin had expected to be done before they arrived. She found Hooker's presence, his hammering sounds, and knocks at the door a disturbance to the privacy she had thought to have in a quiet country house.

And it seemed he was always around. Sometimes Mrs.

Astin felt he was deliberately stalling for time as he puttered slowly at his tasks. She could not imagine why he should stall, but she felt that he did. Even when he was done for the day she would come upon him lingering around the porch or the backyard. It made her nervous, and she was always glad to see his old Ford driving away at last.

"I understood everything would be fixed before we came," the children heard their mother say on the telephone to Mr. Parker at the real estate office.

What Mr. Parker replied they did not know, but Mrs. Astin hung up with a shake of her head. Noticing the children after a moment, she only said, "Well, at least the things are being taken care of now."

But later that day, when Polly and Teddy and Louise were playing outside, Clara was coming downstairs and she chanced to overhear her mother on the phone again. This time she was talking to her husband still at his job in the city far away.

"Mr. Parker apologized, of course," Mrs. Astin was saying. "He said this Mr. Hooker drinks and is sometimes 'indisposed' for a few days."

Clara sat down on the bottom step, cupped her chin in her hands, and listened with interest.

"That's probably why he didn't get over here last week to do these things before we came," Mrs. Astin continued.

There was a pause, and then Mrs. Astin said, "Yes, but Mr. Parker says it's not easy to get odd-jobmen like Mr.

Hooker, so people around here put up with his undependable ways. Eventually he always sobers up and gets back to work. . . . Yes, he's been coming every day, and I've made a list of a few things. There's something wrong with one of the electrical outlets in the living room, which only leaves one at the other end of the room and that's really not sufficient. And several of the windows won't open."

There was another pause as Mr. Astin spoke on the other end of the line. Clara waited.

"Well, yes, I was rather surprised at how old and creaky the house is," her mother said, "but we're getting used to it. . . . Yes, I know the rent was very reasonable. . . . Oh, I'm sure everything will work out all right."

When Mrs Astin hung up the phone, Clara asked at once, "Is Mr. Hooker a *drunk?*"

Mrs. Astin turned with a start. She hadn't heard Clara coming downstairs, and she was sorry Clara had overheard.

"Now don't say anything to the other children, Clara. Apparently he does have a drinking problem, but he is the only one Mr. Parker can get right now, and I'm sure he won't do any drinking around here."

Mrs. Astin struggled with a balky window and gave up in defeat.

"I just wish he'd done all these things before we came. And I certainly wish he would work a little faster. Now that he's finally getting to the work, he seems to take forever to do it."

The children cared even less for Joe Hooker's presence than their mother did. Once Teddy came upon him unexpectedly as he ran around a corner of the house and, looking up, saw the seamed old face high above him and two great arms stretched out.

"Bogeyman will get you!" the raspy voice warned, and Teddy turned and fled, hearing a cruel laugh behind him.

"He looks so mean," Louise told Clara, whispering in the shadows of a tree as they watched Joe Hooker painting porch screens one morning.

Clara considered the hunched figure silently. Why couldn't they have a jolly handyman who would tell them funny stories or whistle while he went about his jobs?

And he *did* seem to take a long time doing things, Clara thought, just as her mother had said. Even now, as he painted the screens, he kept looking up at the house and around the yard . . . as though he were looking for something. Clara followed his gaze toward the house, but she could not see anything unusual, only the curtains at the windows and the trees leaning close.

"Doesn't he look mean?" Louise persisted.

Yes, Clara agreed silently. But she tossed back her dark hair and answered Louise boldly. "He doesn't scare *me*."

A light drizzly rain began to fall early that afternoon, as Joe Hooker drove off in his old car, leaving the painted screens to dry in the backyard shed.

The children had discovered the shed, of course, the

very first day. It stood at the far end of the long backyard, half hidden by trees. Only a few scrubby weeds grew at the sides of the faded walls, and a gnarled dead tree stood like a stark sentinel by the doorway. Inside, the shed was cluttered and dusty, an interesting spot for the children, for they found tools and old boxes, lawnmower parts, a can of half-used dried-up paint, ancient dented oil cans, lengths of rope and wire, yellowing magazines with tattered covers. Clara found pictures of old movie stars in the magazines, and Teddy made a "cave" in one corner with some old boards slanted up against the wall. He would sit under the boards cross-legged, peering smugly out at the others.

On this rainy afternoon the shed was the perfect place to play. Only Louise complained. She sat on the bottom rung of a rickety ladder and chewed an apple and frowned around at all the junk in the shed.

"This isn't any fun," she said.

But the others weren't listening. Polly gazed longingly on Teddy's cave, and Clara was rummaging along a windowsill littered with empty flowerpots and odds and ends of broken china. Unexpectedly, amid the cups without handles and the empty flowerpots, she came upon an old ivory-handled pocketknife and tried to pry open the blades.

"The rain's stopping; let's play somewhere else," Louise murmured restlessly. Through the open shed door she could see Joe Hooker coming out of the back door of the house. She had thought he had gone for the day, and now he might be coming to the shed for something. Louise wasn't going to stay in the shed if he came out there. She wanted to throw her apple core out on the grass for the birds to eat, but she couldn't with Joe Hooker coming.

"This is my cave," Teddy protested to Polly. She had crept along the shed floor on her hands and knees and managed to wiggle herself in under the slanted boards.

"I want to play in here too," Polly said.

"You're taking up all the room."

Polly edged over so she would not take up all the room, and the boards slid down on their heads.

"You broke my cave!" Teddy pushed a board off his leg and it fell against one of the freshly painted porch screens. The screen clattered to the floor—but it was too late to rescue it.

Joe Hooker stood in the shed doorway, glaring in. "Hey, you kids, what're you doing with those screens? And *you*—" Hooker's rough giant hand seemed to come out of nowhere and closed around Clara's. She stared up with fright at the deep-lined face, and the old pocket-knife she had found glinted dully in the light as he pried her fingers open.

For a moment he seemed angry and disappointed to see only the rusting old knife. His hand closed around it as though he would crush it, and then he flung it away with disgust. It hit the floor and skidded into a cobwebby corner, and Polly, pushing her way out from under the tangle of boards, sent another screen clattering to the floor. Dust blew up as the screen slammed down.

"You're ruinin' all my work!" Hooker swung around fiercely. "You kids get on out of here."

Louise, clutching her apple core, was already safely by the door.

"We can play here if we want to," Clara spoke up. But even she was backing away from the angry face.

"Get on out, all of you." Hooker motioned at Polly and Teddy. Teddy's foot came down through a screen as he stumbled past and a gaping hole appeared in the fine mesh of wires.

Louise fled, and Clara caught Polly's hand, dragging the little girl along after her.

"Who wants to play in that old shed anyway," Clara called back defiantly over her shoulder. She saw Hooker standing in the doorway, shaking his fist at them as they scattered away across the yard.

"But he yelled at us so loud," Polly wailed, trailing after her mother in the kitchen.

"It's not *his* shed," Clara said. "It's ours, isn't it? Like the house?"

"Oh . . . I suppose so . . ." Mrs. Astin answered distractedly. Now that the shower was over, she wanted to drive into town. She was hunting for her shopping list, and the children had all come tumbling into the kitchen at the wrong time.

"Try not to get in his way," she said. "When he gets things fixed he won't come except to mow the grass once a week."

There was her shopping list, under the dish towel. She was sure she had not put it there. It was just one of those days when nothing seemed to go right, and now here were all the children fussing around her.

"Go and wash your face and hands, Teddy. You can all come into town with me. That shed's too dirty for you to play in anyway."

"But I had a cave . . ." Teddy tried to explain.

Mrs. Astin had already gone out of the kitchen. She had misplaced her handbag now . . . she was sure she had left it in the living room . . . things kept getting out of place in this house. . . .

Mrs. Astin hated to admit it, but already she was beginning to think she would actually be glad when their two months' vacation was *over*.

CHAPTER THREE

The town was about a mile from the house, and as Mrs. Astin drove along the quiet winding road she began to feel better.

"I have some grocery shopping to do," she said. Smiling into the rearview mirror at Polly, she added, "And let's see if we can find a pretty bowl for those wildflowers you find in the woods, Polly. We'll put it on that table in the middle of the living room. That will brighten up the house, won't it?"

Clara thought it would take a lot more than a bowl of Polly's wildflowers to brighten up that house. She gazed out of the car window and wished she could forget the panic she had felt as Joe Hooker's fingers wrenched away the old pocketknife.

How angry he had been. What did he think she had found? Clara couldn't imagine.

They had finished the grocery shopping and bought a

round red bowl for Polly's flowers and were walking back to the car when Teddy spied the pet shop. There were puppies in the window, soft brown ones with big shining eyes.

"Look at the puppies!" Teddy ran ahead and braced his palms against the glass.

Clara lingered behind a moment at the window of a bookstore next door, but the others followed Teddy to the pet-shop window. Mrs. Astin stood behind Teddy. He twisted his head around and looked up at her hopefully. "Can we have a puppy, Mama?"

Mrs. Astin shook her head regretfully. "No, I don't think so, Teddy."

In the other window were canary cages.

"Can we have a birdie?" Polly begged. "It could sing to us."

Mrs. Astin looked at the canaries. There *was* something bright and happy about them as they flitted about in the cages. Mrs. Astin had had a pet canary when she was a girl, and she remembered the sweet trills of song that had echoed through the house.

"Please, Mama." Polly tugged at her skirt.

"Let's go in and see how much they are," Mrs. Astin said. A canary might be just the right touch for that gloomy old house, she thought to herself. And it would be nice to have one to take back to the city with them at the end of the summer.

Clara came along from the bookstore window, and Teddy was begging, "But I want a puppy," as Mrs. Astin opened the door of the pet shop and went in.

24

A bell tinkled when the shop door opened, and a plump white-haired woman in a blue smock appeared from a room at the back.

"Good afternoon," she said pleasantly. "What can I do for you?"

"I want a puppy," Teddy said to his mother, but she wasn't paying any attention.

"We were looking at the canaries," Mrs. Astin began. She was still trying to make up her mind whether she should buy one.

The plump woman nodded. "Yes, aren't they pretty," she said.

Mrs. Astin followed the woman to the window where the canary cages were, and the children clustered behind. Teddy's bottom lip stuck out sadly.

"We're trying to brighten up a house," Mrs. Astin said with a somewhat apologetic smile. "A canary might be just the thing."

"They're very cheerful little birds," the plump woman agreed. "And they're no trouble."

She lifted one of the cages and the tiny yellow bird inside flitted from perch to perch.

"Don't be frightened," Louise said to it softly. It would be fun to have a little bird like that, she thought. Maybe she could teach it to eat seed from her hand.

But Mrs. Astin still wanted a few minutes to make up her mind. "We've rented a cottage on Old Oak Road," she said. "Just for July and August, and of course it *is* furnished, but we've been out buying a few things to brighten it up." She shifted the package with the new bowl in her arms and nodded toward the bag Clara was carrying, which had the new kitchen curtains in it.

"Oh . . . *that* cottage . . ." The shopkeeper's voice faded away, as though she were not sure what else to say.

"You know the house?" Mrs. Astin asked.

The plump woman smiled faintly. "Everybody knows that house. I mean . . ." She hesitated and then finished lamely, "I mean, it's sort of a landmark. The old Toman house. One of the oldest houses around here."

I can believe that, Clara thought.

"It's spooky," Polly said trustingly. She gazed up at the plump woman with round blue eyes.

The woman looked down at Polly. "You're not the first one who's thought so, I guess," she said consolingly.

"What do you mean?" Mrs. Astin frowned nervously.

"Oh, it's nothing really," the shopkeeper said hastily. "It's just that, well, you know how gloomy those old houses are sometimes, small windows and all."

"Not much sunlight," Mrs. Astin agreed. She shifted her package again. The bowl was growing heavier and heavier to hold, and she suddenly felt hot and tired. She wished she were sitting someplace cool drinking iced tea.

The canary walked around on the cage floor, scattering seed and blinking at the cage bars with bright tiny eyes.

Clara watched the shopkeeper curiously. She had a feeling there was more the woman could say about the house. But not to them. They had already rented it for the whole summer. It was too late to tell them anything about it now.

The shopkeeper smoothed the front of her smock with a plump pink hand. "I'm sure you'll be able to fix the place up real nice," she said. "And it can't be too quiet or gloomy with all these children running in and out."

She reached down and patted Polly's head. "What's your name?"

She's just trying to change the subject, Clara thought. She wished the plump lady would say more about the house.

"This is Polly," Mrs. Astin said, and she turned to see where Teddy was. He was close behind her, still sad because they were going to buy a canary and not a puppy. "This is Teddy. They're twins."

"Isn't that nice," the shopkeeper said with enthusiasm. "Twins. That's a very special thing to be, isn't it?" She smiled down into Polly's upturned face.

"This is Clara," Mrs. Astin added politely, "and this is Louise."

The plump woman smiled at the two older children. "I have a granddaughter just about your age," she said to Clara.

"Clara was thirteen last month," Mrs. Astin said.

"And we had cake," Polly boasted. "A cake *this* big." She held her little arms as far apart as they could go.

"I'm eleven," Louise said shyly. She stood with her hands in the pockets of a pair of Clara's outgrown blue jeans.

"And how many candles did you have on *your* last birthday cake?" the woman asked Polly.

"Six."

"My goodness." The woman nodded as though she were very impressed.

Mrs. Astin brought her attention back to the canaries. "Well, children, what do you think? Shall we buy a canary?"

"Yes, yes," Polly chanted.

"I want a puppy," Teddy said one last time.

"And we'll need a cage, too," Mrs. Astin said. "And some seed."

"And cuttlebone," the shopkeeper added. "Always keep a fresh piece of cuttlebone in the cage."

She shuffled some things around on the counter and found a pamphlet that told all about canaries. "You take one of these along and it'll tell you everything you need to know about keeping a canary. They're easy pets, and I know you'll be glad you decided to get one. They're very cheery to have around."

"My husband thought a house like this would be a good change for us, away from the city and all." Mrs. Astin somehow felt she must explain how they had happened to rent the old house on Old Oak Road. "He came out through this way by himself on business last spring and just happened to see the For Rent sign. He talked to the real estate office and had it all rented and everything taken care of before he even told us."

"He wanted to surprise us," Polly said.

"Yes, and it was a nice surprise, wasn't it," Mrs. Astin said as brightly as she could. "It just needs a few touches. Men don't notice the things that women do, like whether a house is gloomy or not. He just knew there were

28

enough bedrooms and a big front porch and lots of woods around for the children to play in. He's going to join us in a few weeks."

"I wish he was here now," Louise said softly.

The shopkeeper was wrapping up a parcel with canary seed and cuttlebone. Clara watched her face, but the woman kept her eyes down, as if she didn't want to talk about the house anymore.

CHAPTER FOUR

A few days later the children discovered the hidden room under the shed.

They had gone to the shed to play, feeling safe because their mother had told them Joe Hooker was not coming to do any work that day. All the painted screens were now out of the way, hung in their place on the front porch, and Teddy and Polly built their cave again with the old boards.

"I better help you this time," Clara offered, "so it won't all come falling down again."

Louise leaned against the doorframe and looked into the shadowy shed. When she looked outside long enough, into the sunlight, and then looked back into the shed, she could hardly see anything. It was as though the shed grew darker when she wasn't watching. When her eyes got used to the dim light and she could see the others fixing the boards in the corner of the shed, she looked out into the sunlight again until her eyes got used to that.

Being absorbed in this light-and-shadow game, Louise missed the discovery of the trapdoor. Teddy and Polly had dragged a faded piece of carpet across the shed floor to put in their cave, and underneath the spot where the rug had been was the trapdoor. Clara stared down at it with interest: a steel ring fastened into the floor and the square outlines of a door. She knelt down on the dusty shed floor and tugged at the ring.

"Louise," she called with mounting excitement. "I found a trapdoor."

Louise came a few feet into the shed, still blinded by the sunlight.

"Come on," Clara called urgently. "Help me."

Teddy and Polly gave up dragging the carpet to their cave and came to hang over Clara as she lifted the door.

Cool air came up and blew across the children's faces as the door creaked open and they leaned forward to look into the darkness below.

"We need a light." Clara's dark eyes searched the shed. Finding nothing, she tore off for the house to get a flashlight. There was one in a kitchen drawer, and better yet, Mrs. Astin was nowhere in sight. Clara thought her mother would ask why she wanted a flashlight, and then probably tell her not to go down through the trapdoor.

"Stay back. You don't want to fall in." Louise, on

guard in Clara's absence, drew the twins away from the hole in the floor.

"What's down there?" Teddy wanted to know.

Louise knelt and felt cautiously around at the edges of the opening. "It feels like a ladder."

"Don't fall in." Polly's voice wavered.

Then Clara, breathless and flushed, was back with the flashlight.

One by one they went down a narrow ladder and found themselves in a small musty room with an earth floor. Around them were cobwebby shelves holding dark jars, half-burned candles, and small boxes layered with dust. There was a table at one side of the room, a single candle upon it, thick at the base with globs of wax drippings.

A threadbare sort of curtain had been crudely nailed over one wall. Its sagging surface was sewn with a circle of black stars surrounding a dark moon.

Clara moved the light slowly along the shelves and up to the ceiling, where long strands of something weedlike hung down like grasping fingers. She then moved the light on across the floor, and the beam revealed a circle several feet in width etched into the hard ground. It made Clara think of the circles that witches drew and then stood inside of to cast their magic spells . . . but of course there were really no such things as witches.

Over the whole room there seemed to be a deepness of shadow and an eerie stillness.

And then something rustled nearby.

"What was that?" Louise's eyes widened with alarm. "A mouse?"

They listened, but the rustling sound had stopped. The silence afterward seemed somehow just as bad.

"I want to go up," Polly said, suddenly beginning to cry.

"There's nothing to be afraid of," Clara said staunchly.

"I want to go up." Polly smeared at the tears that trembled down her cheeks.

"All right, but be careful." Clara held the light on the rungs of the ladder. She began to feel guilty about letting the twins come down. She should have come first, in case there were mice and things. There was certainly something odd about the room. It wasn't just an extra storage place for tools.

"You go up, too, Teddy," she said. "Go fix your cave some more. And listen," she called after them as they scrambled back up to the shed, "don't tell anybody we found this place. Maybe we'll fix it up and have it for our secret meeting place, and we don't want that old Mr. Hooker to find out about it."

Polly's tear-smudged face appeared beside Teddy's at the edge of the trapdoor.

"Remember, don't tell anyone," Clara repeated. "And leave the rug where it is so we can cover up the door again."

Clara and Louise listened. They could hear the twins' footsteps overhead on the shed floor.

"Let's use this box for a chair," they heard Teddy

33

saying. Then they heard the sounds of something being pushed laboriously across the shed floor.

"What do you think this circle is for?" Clara whispered to Louise. She threw the light across the floor again, and they both stood staring down at the mark on the ground.

"I don't know," Louise said nervously. She twisted her hair and listened for mice.

It's like a witch's circle," Clara said in a low voice.

"What's that?" Louise felt a tremor go up her spine.

"You know, where they stand to do their magic."

Louise looked uneasily at the circle in the dirt.

"And all these jars . . . Clara left the sentence unfinished as she moved the light along the dingy shelves. She lifted a jar and rubbed at the dusty label.

The glass felt cold in her hands, and her fingers trembled as she read the label in the glow of the flashlight beam.

Louise stood close to her, and one by one, as Clara rubbed the dust from the dark jars, they read:

> Blood of Bat
> Tongue of Dog
> Serpent's Tooth
> Rat's Tail
> Eye of Toad
> Dove Hearts
> Spider Heads
> Nightshade
> Powder of Life
> . Powder of Death

And one last jar, where a grayish, clumpy dust glimmered through the dark glass:

Mandrake Root

They heard their mother calling the twins, and they heard the twins run out of the shed.

"Let's go, Clara," Louise begged.

But Clara couldn't leave yet, she was too intrigued.

In the boxes were tiny wax figures, and chains with tufts of fur hanging from them, and queer heavy rings, and animals' teeth, and feathers from birds, and the dead bodies of beetles and flies and spiders with stiff hairy legs.

CHAPTER FIVE

That night after supper Clara and Louise had a secret meeting in their bedroom.

Clara sat cross-legged on the bed, her long dark hair tumbled about her shoulders. Outside the twilight was deepening, and a sultry heat hung in the air. The twins were chasing fireflies in the yard below, and Mrs. Astin sat on the porch swing, wishing her husband had not rented this dark old house.

"We ought to get a book and try some experiments with that stuff," Clara said. She leaned close to thin little Louise. "There's candles there and everything."

"What kind of experiments?"

"Like witches do."

"I don't know . . . " Louise's face was shadowed in the dusky light of the bedroom. She did not feel very adventuresome.

"What harm can it do?" Clara urged.

Louise twisted a strand of hair and wished she were home. She didn't like this summer house. And she didn't like that room under the shed.

"There's mice there."

"Oh, pooh." Clara tossed her dark hair. "They never come out when people are around."

"They might," Louise said, unconvinced.

"They *won't*," Clara insisted.

But Louise was not so sure. Even after she had gone to bed she lay awake and thought about that room under the shed, and the jars and boxes, and the rustling sound she had heard.

The heat that had settled over the countryside the day before was even more oppressive the next morning. The sky was gray, and Mrs. Astin said a storm was coming.

"It's so still," she said with a shake of her head. "I'm glad this isn't tornado country."

"This is the way it gets before a tornado," Clara said with authority. "I read that."

Mrs. Astin smiled to herself. Clara and her books.

"I don't think they ever have tornadoes around here," Mrs. Astin said, scooping pancakes onto plates. "But it is likely to rain before the day's over."

"Louise and I wanted to walk to town and look around," Clara said. In her pocket she had the four dollars of her allowance she had saved. That ought to be enough for a book. "Can we, if we hurry before the rain comes?"

37

Louise poured syrup on her pancakes. Maybe it would rain and she wouldn't have to go to town with Clara to get a book about witches.

Mrs. Astin frowned out at the weather. "I don't think you should go today," she said.

Clara's heart sank.

Louise ate her pancakes with relief. Then she went into the living room and poked her thin fingers through the bars of the canary's cage, talking gently. "Hello, there . . . hello, there . . . "

But by early afternoon no rain had come, and Clara asked again.

"I want to go too," Teddy begged. "I want to go to town with Clara."

Mrs. Astin was tempted. It would mean a quiet hour or two, and she had some letters to write.

"All right, you can all go if you don't take too long. I think the rain will hold off for a while."

She gave them money for ice-cream cones, and waved as they started off down the road. Clara was marching in the lead, with Polly and Teddy fluttering around her like moths. Only Louise turned rather forlornly and waved back.

Clara remembered exactly where the bookshop was, and once she had shepherded the others along to the right street, she let Polly and Teddy run on to look in the pet-shop windows.

"You stay with them," Clara directed Louise. "They

can look at the puppies while I buy the book."

"What if there aren't any books about witches?"

"Well, there *ought* to be." Clara frowned. She had not thought of this possibility. Her hand gripped the knob of the bookshop door. "Bookstores have books about everything," she insisted, and disappeared into the shop.

Louise wandered slowly to the pet-shop window, keeping one eye on the bookstore. She didn't want to lose Clara. She wasn't sure she knew the way back home by herself.

The bookstore was not very large. Narrow aisles traced their way between tables and shelves, and Clara looked around with confusion. A man was paying for a purchase at the front counter, and he went out past Clara without a glance.

"May I help you?" A young woman behind the counter smiled politely at Clara.

Clara hated to ask. It would sound so strange, she thought. But she spoke up as confidently as she could. "Do you have any books about witches?"

"Witches?" the woman repeated with a faint air of surprise. "I don't know for sure. Let's take a look."

She came out from behind the counter and Clara followed her along one of the narrow aisles.

"This is the section on the occult." The young woman paused at a shelf near the back of the store and ran a plum-polished fingernail along the bindings of the books there.

"Mmmm, mmmm," she kept murmuring to herself.

Clara didn't know what "occult" meant. It didn't sound like what she wanted. But then the woman took a book from the shelf.

"Here we are. You're in luck, it seems to be the last one."

The woman dusted the cover with her fingertips before handing it to Clara. "It's been here a while. We don't get many calls for books about witches."

The book was thin, and Clara's hopes rose. It couldn't be very expensive then, she thought.

On the front cover the title was printed in scrolled letters with curlicue tails that would have been difficult to read if the title had not been so simple:

THE BOOK OF WITCHES

Clara flipped through the pages. If it was the only book the woman had on the subject, it would have to do. Words flashed by, along with spidery drawings of medieval cities and barking dogs and crones bending over caldrons in the moonlight.

"We saw the puppies!" Teddy was suddenly there at her elbow, warm and excited, his shirt hanging out of his trousers.

Clara closed the book protectively. Why didn't she *ever* have any privacy!

"How much is this?"

"It should be marked inside," the woman said. She patted Teddy's head. "How are you, young man?"

Teddy dodged behind Clara shyly.

Clara opened the book again, and there, penciled on the first page, was $2.98. Why, she would have more than enough money.

But she hesitated. She hadn't had much of a chance to see if the book was what she really wanted—if it told about how to mix magic potions and cast spells.

"Now if you're interested in anything about astrology, or– Now let me see, we have several books on hypnotism." The young woman misunderstood Clara's hesitation and began to look along the shelf again.

"Oh, no, this is all right," Clara said in desperation. Louise was breathing on the back of her neck, she stood so close trying to see what Clara had found, and Teddy was bumping her leg and Polly was tugging at her skirt. It was hopeless to try to examine the book further.

"Can we get our ice-cream cones now, Clara?" Polly pulled at Clara's arm.

With the others milling around her, Clara made her way back along the aisle, fumbling for her carefully hoarded allowance money.

"Are you going to buy that?" Louise whispered with a last diminishing hope.

But Clara was counting out her money and didn't answer.

Louise watched as the quarters and nickels clinked out.

"What're you buying, Clara?" Polly rested her chin on the counter.

"Oh, nothing . . . " Clara started to say.

41

But the young woman behind the counter was smiling at Polly's rosy face. "A book about witches," she said, making her voice playfully mysterious.

Polly looked up at Clara trustingly.

"You know, there used to be a witch around here once," the woman continued companionably. "At least so the story goes."

"A *real* witch?" Teddy's face brightened with interest.

"I was a witch last Halloween," Polly chirped. "Wasn't I, Clara?"

"A *real* witch?" Teddy persisted. "Did you really see her?"

The woman behind the counter nodded her head solemnly. "Yes, I did."

"What did she look like?" Teddy's eyes bulged.

"Well, she was very tall and strong-looking for an old woman, and she had gray hair in a big knot on the back of her head. I don't know if she looked like a witch or not, but a lot of people around here thought she *was* a witch."

"Why did they think so?"

"Just strange things that happened. They said she was always out prowling in the woods at night, hunting for things to make potions with. And they said it was bad luck to meet her on the street when she came to town."

The woman paused, thinking back. "She didn't come to town often, but I remember my mother used to say she could always tell when the old woman was coming. We had a dog named Ginger, and I remember sometimes when I came home from school my mother would say, 'Look at Ginger—that woman's in town today.' And sure enough, Ginger would be sitting by our front window, ears cocked as if she were listening for something. She was usually a very gentle dog, but she'd sit there by the window and growl low in her throat. And she wouldn't touch her food all day."

The woman put Clara's book into a crinkly green paper bag as she talked.

"Boys from town used to fish in a stream in the woods near her house, and they said she would come and stand by the trees and just stare at them. One day one of the boys shouted at her, 'We can fish here; you don't own this stream.' And after that nobody ever caught another fish in that stream. They were all gone."

Clara thought of the stream by their house, where they had taken picnic lunches. . . . She thought of Teddy wading at the edge of the bank, scooping his hands down into the shallow water. "I'm going to catch a fish," he would call. But he never did.

"And then there was Mr. Tucker," the woman continued. "I saw that myself. I was in his hardware store one day when the old woman came in. Everyone always got very quiet when she was around. They'd stop talking and sort of bunch together, away from her. Well, anyway, she told Mr. Tucker she wanted some twine, and when he gave her her change, she said he had cheated her. Mr. Tucker said he hadn't. She stood and looked at him— I suppose it was only a moment or two, but it seemed like a long time. Her eyes seemed to pierce right through him. And then she left without another word. Mr. Tucker was always sickly after that, and everyone said the old witch had put a curse on him."

The children listened in awed silence.

Then Teddy asked curiously, "What happened to her?"

"She died about seven or eight years ago. Actually it was rather strange . . . " The woman shook her head thoughtfully. "You see, everyone thought she was very poor. She always wore a long worn-out black coat, and she never spent much money when she came into town to buy food and things. But when she died she left her house and her 'treasure' to a cousin who lived here in town. After she died they found a letter she'd written, and that's the way she put it, 'my house and my treasure.' But her cousin never found any treasure, and finally he sold the house. No one knows if there ever really was a treasure or not.

"The house has changed hands a couple of times since then. Nobody ever seems to want to stay there very long. The last family who bought the house moved away and left it in the hands of a real estate agency here in town, to sell or rent or do with whatever they could. I don't know if they'll be able to do anything with it. People here in town say it's haunted, that it still has a spell over it from when old Bertha Toman lived there."

Bertha *Toman*. Poor Louise felt her heart racing. The woman at the pet shop had called their house "the old Toman house."

44

But Teddy didn't remember that. "What was her house like?" He pressed close against the counter and stared up at the woman.

"Small and old. Not particularly unusual, really. Maybe you've seen it, out on Old Oak Road. It's almost hidden by trees, but you can see it if you know where to look. It's painted dark brown, and there's a big front porch and an old shed and lots and lots of trees."

"That's our house," Polly piped up. "Our daddy rented it."

The young woman looked surprised. "Oh?" she said uncertainly. Then she leaned forward across the counter and touched Polly's face gently. "Don't worry, those are just old tales. Just town gossip. I'm sure it's a very nice house."

The children left the bookshop and walked home along Old Oak Road silent and subdued.

Above them the sky remained gray and ominous, and now there were rumbles of thunder in the distance.

It was going to storm, just as their mother had said. Hardly a leaf moved in the still, sultry heat of the afternoon.

CHAPTER SIX

Mrs. Astin had spent the time the children were gone writing a few letters to friends back home.

It's a rather queer little house, but the children are enjoying themselves. . . . There's a nice swimming pool in town. . . . The children love the woods. . . .

As the afternoon grew darker, Mrs. Astin lighted lamps in the lower rooms and watched for the children's return. The threatening storm made her uneasy, and she was about to get into the car and drive to town after them when they came at last, up the road and through the trees, a strung-out file of wanderers.

"You're back just in time," she greeted them cheerfully. "I'm going to make a cake for supper, and I know somebody who likes to lick frosting bowls."

"Me!" Polly said, lifting her face for a kiss.

"You?" Mrs. Astin smoothed the soft golden hair and

looked deep into Polly's eyes. "I never would have guessed."

"Mama, Mama." Teddy shouted for attention. "A lady told us a witch used to live here."

"A witch?"

"Clara bought a book, and the lady told us:"

So then Clara had to show the book. It was so hard to keep secrets! Next the twins would probably tell about the room under the shed.

But Mrs. Astin only glanced at the book.

"I can't imagine why you want to read such stuff," she said a bit impatiently. Clara was always spending her allowance money on books, so there was nothing unusual about that. But the house was gloomy enough without all this talk of witches.

"Do you think a witch lived here, Mama?" Teddy asked.

"No, of course not, dear," Mrs. Astin said, trying to regain her cheerfulness. "Now come and help me make the cake."

"The lady said she used to hunt for things in the woods," Teddy chattered on, following his mother and Polly to the kitchen.

"Is that so?" Mrs. Astin set out measuring spoons and a flour sifter. From the kitchen window she could see the woods, bleak and mysterious under the stormy sky.

"And after she died, everybody thought her house was haunted."

Mrs. Astin thought of the shadows in the corners of the rooms where the lamplight didn't reach . . . and she set out the mixing bowl with an air of determined good cheer that she did not quite feel.

Clara and Louise went upstairs and sat on the edge of their bed with *The Book of Witches* open between them, leafing through the pages like conspirators while the thunder grew closer.

Clara's quick look through the book at the bookstore had revealed little, and she found now, with a quickening heartbeat, that she had before her all that she had hoped, a book of sorcery, incantations, and ancient lore. She did not hear when the rain started at last, pelting against the windowpanes of the tiny bedroom, as she read of witches burned at the stake, of sabbats on crossroads where no grass grew ever after, of spirits summoned from the underworld, of skies turning black at midday, and of dogs howling at the approach of a witch.

A darkening sky and rising wind foretell the coming of a witch. In ancient towns dogs howled and the children were called in from play. A field where a witch had crossed would yield no crop again, and it was believed that plague struck anyone on whom the shadow of a witch had fallen. . . .

The words shimmered upon the page, and Clara drew in her breath. Louise leaned against her shoulder, and stared at the picture of a cellar crawling with spiders and snakes . . . but Clara was already turning on. The pages rustled softly in the lamplight.

In fire is my power, in numbers is my power, in the circle is my power, Clara read, dark eyes glowing.

Louise could not read as fast as Clara, and she didn't understand all the words. Before she had finished puzzling over one page, Clara was turning on to the next one.

Cats, owls, and ravens were the most common familiars of the witches, traveling with them as companions and servants, prisoners of unholy incantations against which they were powerless. . .

There was a drawing of a great black bird perched on the shoulder of a horrid scraggly-haired hag whose face stared out at Louise and made her heart grow cold.

But Clara raced on to another page.

Standing within the magic circle drawn upon the ground with a sharp pointed stick, the witch could call down sickness, fire, earthquake, flood, famine, and death, as she brooded with her horny hands and sprinkled her evil brews upon the earth. Magic charms were worn to ward off the wicked spells of witches, but there were witches who knew how to take the magic from those charms, rendering their victims helpless after all. . . .

Another page. And another. And the rain beat down upon the old house and the afternoon wore on toward evening. Descriptions of spells, hexes, secret potions; lists of chants; tales of the power of candles made from human fat—all were in the pages, in the lamplight.

"Listen to this." Clara began to read aloud with a feverish excitement: *"When it is necessary for a witch to pass through a material object such as a door or a wall, she must hold the teeth of a cat in her right hand, the teeth of a serpent in her left hand, and say:*

" 'I call upon the powers of the known and the unknown. I call upon cat and serpent. I call upon the seven powers of thunder and fire and earthquake.'

"Then she will pass through whatever obstacle is present. There is no safety from witches, who can thus enter locked rooms and escape from barred cells!"

Clara lifted her eyes and stared with awe at Louise.

Poor Louise felt as though at that very moment a witch would come through the floor beneath her feet and appear before them with wild hair and ragged claws, casting upon Louise the tooth of a cat and the tooth of a snake.

"And listen to this." Clara began to read again, rapidly: *"It is necessary for a witch to secure the blood of bats by visiting their caves at the time of the full moon. She must seize the bat by its wings and take the blood from its neck into her vial."*

There was no picture on that page, but in Louise's imagination bat-hung cave walls glimmered in a ghostly moonlight—and then there was a shrieking and flying and battering of wings as the witch came into their midst.

"I want to find something *we* can do." Clara began to turn through the pages more quickly, mumbling over the paragraph headings:

"*Love Potions . . . To Protect a House Against Devils . . . To Move Objects . . .*" She kept shaking her head.

Transformation of a Cat: By the seven powers of the seven fires I will change thee. By the blood of goats and eyes of newts, I will change thee. By the touch of fur and the touch of fire, I will change thee. . . .

Clara hesitated. But she had no cat to transform. And what were newts?

She turned on to more pages.

"*Boil a two-headed lizard in oil, anoint the victim, and he will die,*" she read aloud.

"Oh, Clara — " Louise huddled closer. "Let's not do that one."

"No," Clara agreed with a shiver, "we won't do that one."

Louise leaned closer over the book; from its pages an essence of undefined evil rose and engulfed her.

"*Disappearances.*" Clara read aloud. "*The witches of the seventeenth century perfected the magic of disappearances past any previous ability of witches. Entering her magic circle, tracing within it a smaller circle, the witch placed within that smaller circle a mixture of mandrake root and pure earth and some personal possession of the person (or in the case of an animal, a tuft of fur, or a tooth, etc.), and began her chant:*

51

*"By the seven powers of the seven powers of darkness,
I will make you disappear. Mandrake root and pure
earth; I will make you disappear. All that is known to
the darkness and the seven powers of the seven darknesses take you, take you, take you."*

Clara looked up, her eyes burning with intensity upon
Louise. "There's a mandrake root in one of those jars,"
she whispered. She felt the hand of fate upon her.

"I don't think we should do *that*," Louise protested
fearfully.

"Not a real person," Clara said. "Maybe something
like a cat or a dog."

Louise stared into Clara's eyes hypnotically. "But we
don't have a cat or a dog."

Clara paused uncertainly, glancing back at the page.
The words seemed to rise from the page toward her. *I will
make you disappear . . . the seven powers of the seven
darkness . . . This* was the magic she wanted to try. But
it was true, they had no cat or dog.

Louise curled her slim arms around her knees protectively. "Let's try to make a charm against evil powers,"
she said timidly. It sounded safer, she thought. And in
this strange, small dark house it would be good to have
something to ward off evil, in case a witch really had
lived here once and her evil spell remained somehow.

But Clara was hardly listening.

"We have a canary," she whispered.

Louise felt cold, and she hugged her knees tighter.

52

"Nobody would really miss it," Clara said.

"I would."

"We could buy another one afterward."

Below, from the kitchen, they could hear the voices of the twins as they begged for the frosting bowl to lick.

"You can each have a spoon." Their mother's voice came up to the bedroom faintly, as though from a long, long way off. "I hope you won't spoil your appetites for supper."

All night rain streamed down the windows of the house. The trees tossed wildly in the darkness, casting eerie shadows as the lightning crackled. Thunder rumbled close overhead.

Clara lay in bed listening to the storm and thinking about what the woman in the bookstore had said. If the witch really had left a treasure, maybe she and Louise could find it even if no one else had. But where could they look that everybody hadn't probably already looked?

And tomorrow she had something more important to do. She thought about the witch's room below the shed, with its bottles and candles and the magic circle on the floor. She would have to bring a sharp stick, she thought, to make the circle plainer (it was so old and half disappearing) and to make the smaller circle within it. She would need mandrake root and pure earth. And a feather from the canary.

Would it hurt the canary if she pulled out a feather?

53

Under her pillow was *The Book of Witches*, where no one could find it and read it except Clara and Louise. And if the canary really did disappear, they would never tell. They had sworn to that.

Louise listened to the storm too, and when she fell asleep at last she dreamed of a bats' cave filled with the shrieking of bats and the rush of their wings, of witches with hair that reached to the ground, of thunder rumbling and echoing in the cave, and of the sound of blood dripping like hard rain upon a roof.

CHAPTER SEVEN

It was quite easy to get a canary feather—easier than Clara had dared hope. She did not even have to pluck the canary. Several small yellow feathers lay on the floor of the birdcage.

Clara opened the cage door furtively, and the canary flew upward away from her hand and clung to the bars of the cage.

Louise, keeping watch at the living-room window, shifted anxiously from foot to foot. The rain was over, but the morning was cloudy and cool. In the front yard Mrs. Astin and the twins were setting up an old croquet set they had found in a closet of the house. Mrs. Astin paced off distances in the damp grass and stuck the wickets down while Polly and Teddy got in each other's way knocking at the croquet balls with paint-chipped mallets. There was no one in sight on the road beyond.

A squirrel watched from a tree branch. Louise watched from behind the curtain.

"Hurry up," she pleaded with Clara.

"I've got them." Clara clasped the cage door securely back into place.

Louise left her post at the window to come and examine the two small yellow feathers.

"Do you think they're big enough?"

"I don't think it matters how big they are," Clara said, "as long as they belong to the canary."

Louise looked through the cage bars, and two bright beady eyes stared back at her.

They went out the back way, through the kitchen. When they were halfway across the backyard, Clara gave Louise the feathers to hold and ran back to the kitchen for matches for the candles. Louise waited, feeling the wet spiky grass at the tops of her sandals and her heart beating fast inside her.

The hidden room below the shed lay in a gloom of decay and despair. The candle Clara had lighted on the table flickered palely upon the open pages of the book.

Louise shrank close to the candlelight, while Clara traced the circle more clearly in the ground with her pointed stick and then drew within it a smaller circle.

"Mandrake root . . . " Clara ran her finger along the page in *The Book of Witches*, mumbling to herself, and then she took up the candle and moved along the shelves.

"Pure earth—is that just dirt?" Louise asked.

"I guess so." Clara moved the candle farther along the

shelf, searching. "There isn't anything here that says 'pure earth,' so it must be just regular dirt."

"What if it isn't? What if it's some special dirt?"

"Then it won't work, I guess."

"Oh," Louise blinked at the candle flame. Goose bumps tingled on her arms.

Clara did not know what she had expected mandrake root to be like. A knotty clump of gray powder fell into her hand when she tilted the bottle. Louise leaned forward warily to look. But she did not lean too close.

"How much do you need?"

"Oh . . . that ought to be enough." Clara dropped a gray lump into the small circle and brushed her hands clean. She didn't like the feel of it on her fingers.

She scratched up a bit of dirt from the floor by the outer edge of the big circle, and added that to the mandrake root. For good measure, she rubbed at the little pile with her stick to mix it all together.

"Give me the feathers."

Louise opened her hand. She felt cold, but her fingers, which had been clutched tightly around the canary feathers, were clammy with perspiration. The feathers, limp and bedraggled, lay in her palm.

Clara lifted the feathers carefully and squatted down to put them on the top of the mandrake root and pure earth.

"Now we're ready to begin."

She flashed Louise a daring look and stepped boldly into the circle.

The candle fluttered as though a draft had blown

across it, and Louise's heart sank . . . but Clara's face, quivering with shadows in the flame light, held her spellbound. Clara looked like a witch, Louise thought, with her great dark eyes and flowing dark hair. . . .

And then Clara began to chant slowly and solemnly.

"By the seven powers of the seven powers of darkness, I will make you disappear. Mandrake root and pure earth; I will make you disappear. All that is known to the darkness and the seven powers of the seven darknesses take you, take you, take you."

CHAPTER EIGHT

The first thing Clara and Louise saw when they came out of the shed was Joe Hooker's car parked at the side of the house.

They stared with surprise and a quickening sense of having survived a close call. What if Joe Hooker had come to get something from the shed and had found the trapdoor locked from the inside!

"Mama said he wasn't coming today." Clara felt betrayed somehow. Oh, what a chance they had taken!

Louise looked around uneasily. "I wonder where he is?"

They skirted the house cautiously, their footsteps soundless in the damp grass. The front yard was deserted. The croquet wickets stood poked into the ground, the mallets and balls clustered amid the roots of an old tree.

"Everybody must be inside," Clara said. Joe Hooker was certainly nowhere in sight.

The girls stood in the yard under the low, whispering branches of the trees.

"Well," Clara said at last, "let's go in and see if the canary has disappeared."

Louise hung back, twisting her hair. "Oh, that was just a game, Clara. It really wouldn't *work*."

Clara tightened her grip on *The Book of Witches*. She could feel the slightly raised scrolled lettering of the title against her arm. Maybe Mr. Hooker had unexpectedly come to do some work after all, but he hadn't caught them, and she began to have a sense of daring exaltation. *Mandrake root and pure earth . . . I will make you disappear. . . .* Back there, in the witch's room, nothing had seemed to exist around her but the flickering candle flame. It was as though she had stood for a moment in the center of darkness, with the walls of the witch's room gone out away from her into infinite space, infinite darkness, beyond the candlelight. There had been no one but herself in the drawn circle. And the rising flame of the candle.

"Come on." She grasped Louise's hand and started toward the house. "Let's go see if it was only a game or not."

They went up the front-porch steps, Clara pulling Louise, and as they opened the door the sound of Teddy's voice raised in some shrill protest reached them.

"I didn't, I didn't!"

They stood in the hall a moment, listening, and the voice from the living room rose sharply, mingled with Polly's wail:

"I *didn't,* Mama, I *didn't.*"

"Well, someone did." Mrs. Astin's voice was weary with vexation.

Clara and Louise lurked in the living-room doorway, and the first thing Clara saw was that Joe Hooker was there in a corner, kneeling by a light socket with a tool-box open beside him.

"I didn't, I didn't," Teddy protested again. He stood dejectedly by the old sofa, kicking one droopy-laced canvas shoe against the sofa leg.

"Stop that kicking," his mother directed impatiently, and then, to Polly, who had crawled under a small table on her hands and knees, "Get up. It's not under there."

Mrs. Astin caught sight of the older girls in the doorway. "The canary's gone," she explained with a helpless gesture. "Someone must have left the cage door open."

"I didn't, I didn't," Teddy began again.

Mrs. Astin looked at him suspiciously, and Polly bumped her head on the table and began to cry. Mrs. Astin felt the last shreds of patience fleeing from her, but she managed to help Polly up and patted the bumped head soothingly. "There now, Polly, you're all right, don't cry."

Polly saw Clara and Louise. Her mouth turned down and fresh tears welled into her eyes. "Our birdie's gone."

"I can't imagine where it could be," Mrs. Astin said. "We've looked in every room."

Clara's fingers tightened on *The Book of Witches.* She had not expected such a scene of confusion. She had not thought anybody would cry, or that her mother would be so upset. She had not thought of any of those things. And there was Joe Hooker, watching from the corner of his eye, almost as if he *knew*.

Louise shrank closer to Clara. Her cheeks were flushed, and she chewed at her lower lip and twisted her hair.

Mrs. Astin gave one more distracted, searching look around the parlor. "I know there are no windows open —half of them *won't* open." She hoped Joe Hooker would get her meaning in this; he was supposed to have taken care of things like that before they arrived.

Teddy was hanging down to peer under the sofa, his chubby face reddening.

"Well, I've got things to do in the kitchen." Mrs. Astin put an end to the whole matter with a sigh. "Go and wash your face, Polly." Her voice softened. "If the cage door was left open, I suppose it was an accident. The bird is probably behind the furniture somewhere. It will fly out sooner or later."

The children could hear their mother's steps in the hall and then on the kitchen linoleum. They could hear water running in the kitchen sink.

In the silence that settled over the parlor, Clara looked at the empty cage. It hung motionless in its curved holder, outlined against the window with the gray light falling through it like an omen of ill-fortune.

"It's not nice for little children to tell lies."

Joe Hooker stood up, towering above them all, tapping the handle of a screwdriver against one calloused

62

palm. His eyes were squinted, and he shook his head at Teddy and Polly.

Teddy cowered against the sofa, and tears trembled in Polly's eyes.

"They weren't lying," Clara spoke up bravely. She didn't like Joe Hooker talking to the twins like that.

"How do *you* know, Miss Smartie?"

Clara did not know what to say to that. Her eyes met Louise's for a moment, guiltily. But they had sworn never to tell.

"I just know," Clara said as staunchly as she could.

Hooker smiled dryly. "Bad things happen to little children who tell lies," he said to the twins again. "Bad things."

How strange his eyes looked, Louise thought fearfully. Red and watery . . . what was wrong with him?

"We didn't do anything." Teddy edged toward Clara, hypnotized by the face that loomed above him.

"Bad, bad things." Hooker smiled evilly and tapped the screwdriver in his open palm with a steady, ominous beat.

Louise was frantic to get away. "Come on, Polly. Mama said to wash your face."

The children left Hooker there, with the empty cage and the gray light at the windows, but they felt his gaze following them. At the top of the stairs Louise looked back over her shoulder. He was still there in the living room, watching through the doorway.

Clara and Teddy went into the kitchen, and Mrs. Astin

turned from the sink, drying her hands on her apron.

"I don't like that man," Teddy pouted. He stood close to his mother.

Mrs. Astin sighed. "Daddy will be here next week," she said. Clara thought it was as though her mother were also saying "Then everything will be all right."

When Teddy had gone out to the yard, Mrs. Astin confided to Clara, "I think Mr. Hooker has been drinking this morning. I'm going to tell him not to come anymore."

Clara was glad to hear that. "Sure," she agreed. "Daddy can probably fix whatever needs fixing when he comes."

Mrs. Astin turned back to the sink. Even getting things fixed wouldn't help much, she thought to herself. There was no getting around it, the house just wasn't right for them, and she wished her husband had never rented it.

But where *was* that canary? Mrs. Astin had never had so many things go wrong in so short a time in any place she had ever lived before.

"Well," she said with a determined air, "I'll just see if he's fixed that wall outlet. Then I'll have another look upstairs for that bird."

When her mother left the kitchen, Clara opened *The Book of Witches* on the table between a jar of peanut butter and a water glass from which a few flowering weeds Polly had picked sprouted like porcupine quills. She began to look through the book furtively, flipping the pages impatiently. She had not read all of the book yet; maybe she could find something to reverse disappearances and make things come back. She had not expected so much hubbub over one little canary.

CHAPTER NINE

Clara was so intent on her book that she did not hear Louise come into the kitchen.

"Clara . . ."

The soft voice so close to her made Clara jump. *The Book of Witches* slammed closed.

"Clara—do you think we could get the canary back?"

"What do you think I'm trying to do?" Clara felt bad enough without having Louise creep up behind her, whispering as if they were criminals.

"Let's try." Louise leaned closer, glancing over her shoulder to be sure their mother was still with Mr. Hooker in the living room. "Let's see if the book says anything about making things come back."

"I've already looked."

There was a certain gleam in Clara's dark eyes, and Louise felt a sense of burden falling from her. Clara had found something and they would get the canary back!

"What does it say? Let me see."

"Not here." Clara put her fingers to her lips. Already they could hear Polly on her way downstairs with her freshly washed face. "Let's go outside and I'll show you."

Sneaking one more look toward the living room, Louise followed Clara out the back door, and Polly found only a deserted kitchen. Kneeling in a chair by the table, she smelled contentedly at her "flowers."

Clara and Louise found a secluded spot at the side of the backyard and huddled over the book. Teddy had gone around to the front. Now and then they could hear the heavy clonk of a mallet striking a croquet ball.

"Here." Clara riffled through the pages a moment and then thrust the book at Louise, who hung over it so close that her hair brushed against the pages as she read:

APPEARANCES

Standing in the magic circle, the witch sprinkles cat fur and human blood upon the ground. A possession of the missing person is added. "From the unknown, from the faraway places of the darkness, I summon you. Come through fire and earthquake and darkness. I summon you."

Louise read the instructions silently, and then looked up at Clara with disappointment.

"But we haven't got any cat fur."

"We've got to find some," Clara said firmly.

Louise looked doubtful about this. "Where?"

"Maybe we can find a cat somewhere."

67

Louise eyed Clara gravely.

Clara frowned at the book. Why did it have to be cat fur? Why couldn't it be something they *had?* It had been so easy with the mandrake root and pure earth.

Louise was silent a moment.

"Clara."

"What?"

Louise's eyes were on the house, half hidden by trees. "Do you suppose the witch really did leave a treasure?"

"I don't know," Clara answered slowly. Something in the way Louise was looking at the house reminded her of something she couldn't explain for a moment. Then it came to her. Joe Hooker, painting the porch screens, had stopped to stare up at the house just the way Louise was staring now, thoughtfully, with narrowed eyes. Suddenly Clara knew: whether old Bertha Toman had left a treasure or not, Joe Hooker thought she had, and he was looking for it. That was why he was always taking so long to do things, was always hanging around. He was trying to find the treasure.

"Clara?"

Clara started as Louise nudged her from her thoughts.

"Do you think there is a treasure somewhere in that house?"

"Whether there is or not," Clara said with a sigh, "what *we* have to do is find a cat."

Right then, finding a cat seemed harder than finding a treasure.

"Maybe there are some cats in the woods," Louise said hopefully.

"Maybe." Clara closed the book and tried to concentrate. "Or maybe we can walk into town. We might find a stray cat there."

Now that the storm and the cool of the morning had passed, the day was growing hot and sultry again.

"It's awfully warm for a walk into town," Mrs. Astin objected at lunchtime. But finally she said they could go if they wanted to. Clara and Louise exchanged relieved glances across the kitchen table. Then, a moment later, Polly and Teddy began to clamor to go too, and Mrs. Astin said, "Yes, yes—you can all go," which wasn't exactly what Clara and Louise had in mind.

"How are we going to look for a cat with them tagging along?" Louise fretted, changing into a clean blouse that had been Clara's the summer before.

"We'll have to *try*." Clara's voice was full of disappointment. She brushed her hair absently, and Louise, ready in her clean hand-me-down blouse, curled her legs under her in the rocking chair and creaked back and forth with a gloomy expression on her face.

"I'm ready." Polly came running into the bedroom, a ribbon around her head and a doll under her arm.

Clara took one last look at herself in the mirror, closed her eyes for a second, and silently offered up the prayer, "Please let us find a cat."

Then, in case her prayer came true, she put a small pair of scissors in her pocket.

The four walked along in the silent, dull afternoon, Clara and Louise carefully watching both sides of the road, hoping to see a stray cat come out of the woods. It was going to be hard hunting for one with the twins tagging along.

They were only about halfway to town when Louise said, "This isn't going to work. Let's just go home."

The twins had run on a way ahead, and Clara hesitated. "We've got to find a cat *some*place."

"It isn't going to work this way," Louise persisted. "What if we do find a cat. How can we get some fur without the twins seeing? They'll ask questions."

Clara frowned at the woods. Why couldn't a nice plain old cat come slinking along?

But of course Louise was right, and after a moment Clara raised her voice and called the twins. "Hey! We're going home."

"We want to go to town." Polly came running back toward Clara.

"I want to see the puppies in that store," Teddy begged.

"It's too hot to walk all that way," Clara said.

"I'm not hot," Polly declared.

"Well, I am," Clara insisted.

"Me too," Louise agreed. "Mama was right, it's too hot." She turned and marched sturdily beside Clara back toward the house.

The twins trailed behind, and their mother said, "My goodness, home so soon?"

"It was too hot," Clara said.

Mrs. Astin shook her head helplessly. That was what she had tried to tell them.

Polly and Teddy ran off to play in their cave in the shed, and Louise and Clara went upstairs to consult *The Book of Witches* again.

"Maybe we missed something," Clara suggested hopefully.

But a half hour of steady leafing through the pages, past the horrifying pictures and bold black paragraph headings, revealed no further information or incantation about "Appearances" other than the one they had already found.

Over and over Clara turned the pages. *Love Potions . . . Transformations . . . Vampires . . . Hemlock . . . By the seven powers of the seven powers of darkness, I will make you disappear. . . . In fire is my power, in numbers is my power, in the circle is my power. . . . In fire is my power, in numbers is my power, in the circle is my power. . . .*

At last Clara flung the book aside with vexation. She had wanted it so much; she had thought she would try *lots* of experiments. Now it wasn't as much fun as she had thought it would be. She *had* wanted the canary to disappear, but she hadn't expected to feel so queer about it afterward.

"Clara . . ." Louise twisted her hair. "Maybe if that witch really did leave a treasure, like the woman in the bookstore said, well, maybe we could find it."

Clara lifted her dark eyes. She took a deep breath.

"I think we already have."

Louise blinked with surprise.

"I think we already have," Clara repeated. She felt

overcome with the awe of her discovery.

She leaned close to Louise. "The room under the shed was her 'treasure.' "

Louise gazed back at Clara blankly.

"That's *got* to be it, don't you see? And we found it when no one else could—not all those people who have lived in this house since the witch died—because they didn't know what it was when they saw it.

"And you know what else I think?" Clara was whispering now. "I think that mean old Mr. Hooker is looking for the treasure. Haven't you ever noticed how long he always takes to do things, and how he's always poking around afterward. Why doesn't he just go home when he's through with his work? He's looking for the treasure, that's why. He probably thinks it's a bag of money or something like that."

Louise's eyes were as round as saucers.

What I did on my summer vacation.

She wished they were visiting Aunt Esther again. They had seen fireworks and she had won a pink elephant. She didn't really want to live in a witch's house.

The room was silent.

At last Louise took up the book Clara had cast away. She held it as though it might bite her. "Maybe we ought to make some magic charms, you know, in case there's any bad spells left over from when the witch lived here."

Ever since they had bought the book, that had been on her mind.

Clara considered the idea, smoothing her dark hair.

72

Making charms against a witch's power certainly couldn't do any harm.

"What does it say?" She moved closer to Louise and peered down at the open page.

Louise, tracing the lines with a thin finger, read aloud slowly and carefully:

"*Many charms and am-am-*"

"Amulets," Clara prompted.

"*. . . amulets were worn by townsfolk to protect them from the evil of witches. A wolf's tooth carried in a pocket or worn in a shoe was thought to be one of the most effective ways to secure protection.*"

Clara groaned inwardly. Wolves teeth. Cat fur. Why couldn't it be something they *had*.

But Louise was reading on.

"*Another magic tal-talisman was a charm worn around the neck. Pictures were drawn on the charm. Flowers, birds, stars. All these were considered to be symbols of good against which the powers of sorcery were useless.*"

Louise looked up from the book. "We could make those, Clara," she whispered eagerly. "We could make them out of cardboard and put them on strings. I could draw pictures on them."

Clara began to nod thoughtfully. Here was something they could really do. Louise got the best marks for art of anybody in her class at school. Her birds and flowers and stars would be beautiful. Clara stood up slowly, and Louise closed the cover of *The Book of Witches*.

There was no one downstairs. The sunlight had faded,

and an eerie silence seeped from the shadowy corners of the room. The empty birdcage hung motionless by the living-room window. In the kitchen the shadows were even deeper in the waning light, and Louise shivered and hugged herself with her thin arms.

Clara was already searching through the kitchen wastebasket. "Here—this will do." She held up an empty cereal box. There were letters on the outside, but the inside was bare gray cardboard.

"And we need some string." Clara hunted through a kitchen drawer. Maybe if the charms were powerful enough, the canary might even come back!

Clara still had the scissors in her pocket, and they found a box of crayons in Polly's room. Then, in their bedroom, as the trees pressed close to the windows, they began to make their magic charms.

Clara cut out circles of cardboard about the size of silver dollars, picked tiny holes at the edge with the point of the scissors, and measured off lengths of string.

"I'm cutting four," she explained, "because I think we should make charms for Polly and Teddy too."

Louise lay on her stomach across the bed and, using *The Book of Witches* as a hard place to draw on, decorated each cardboard cutout with a picture. She made two flowers and a bird and a star.

As each drawing was finished, Clara carefully strung the circle on a long piece of string and tied it with a knot. When the first magic charm was finished, she put it around her own neck to try it out.

"I think we ought to wear them inside our blouses," she decided. "We don't want everybody asking questions about them. There." She buttoned her blouse again and rearranged her collar. "Can you see anything?"

"Just a little bit of string around your neck." Louise studied Clara with approval. Then, continuing her artwork, she said, "I think Teddy would like the bird. And let's give Polly the star. . . . Oh, but Clara. What will we tell them?" Her crayon hung suspended above the last cardboard circle.

Clara figured a moment. "We'll just say they're good-luck charms we made for fun."

The crayon descended again and the points of the star took shape on the cardboard circle. Polly's magic amulet.

The twins, hot and perspiring in the shed, crawled out from their cave and allowed the cardboard and string to be put around their necks. Polly kept pulling hers up to look at the picture, until Clara said, "You'll have it all worn out, Polly. Besides, it's a *secret* good-luck charm. Nobody's supposed to see it."

Satisfied with their afternoon's work, Clara and Louise headed for the house again, with Polly and Teddy behind them chanting, "Lemonade—lemonade—lemonade."

"What's that around your neck?" Mrs. Astin asked at her first glimpse of little Polly.

Why did mothers have such sharp eyes? Clara and Louise exchanged a worried look. What if their mother made them take off the magic charms?

"Good-luck charms," Polly piped up cheerfully. Her playsuit was dusty from the shed floor, and she had lost her hair ribbon. "Clara and Louise made them."

"I see." Mrs. Astin smiled faintly. She didn't believe in good-luck charms, of course, not anymore, but she could remember when she had been a little girl just about Polly's age and her older brother had given her a lucky penny. She had carried it to school every day in her coat pocket.

"Mine has a bird." Teddy hauled up his cardboard by the string until it had come all the way out of his shirt.

"Very pretty," Mrs. Astin said. She paused a moment as she set out the glasses for the lemonade, and admired the bird. "Louise draws well, doesn't she?"

And that, to the great relief of Clara and Louise, was all that was said about the magic charms.

By the time they went to bed that night, Clara and Louise felt as if the day had been an especially long one. It seemed ages and ages since they had lighted the candle in the shed early that morning and made the canary disappear.

"I'm going to leave the cage door open in case the birdie comes back," Polly said at bedtime. She and Teddy stood in their pajamas by the empty cage.

"Then he can get in and have his seed," Teddy said.

Mrs. Astin sighed. She hated to see the little ones so hopeful, and so sure to be disappointed. As far as Mrs. Astin could see, the canary was *gone*. Somehow it must

76

have gotten out of the cage and escaped through a door that had been left ajar. It would probably not survive long outside, or ever return to its shiny cage.

Clara lay awake listening to hear if the black clock would begin to tick again, but all she could hear was the crickets outside. Once she got up and looked out the window, peering through the trees that groped in upon the house. She could just make out the outline of the shed, silent and dark, far away between the trees, and she thought she could almost see the tall figure of old Bertha Toman stalking the shadows in her long, raggedy black coat.

Clara touched the string around her neck. The canary *had* disappeared. A witch *had* lived here once. It was good to have a magic amulet.

But still, tomorrow, somehow, she and Louise had to find a cat.

CHAPTER TEN

Clara slept late the next morning and ate her breakfast alone in the cheerless kitchen.

A note on the table said:

Hello, sleepyheads. The twins and I have gone to the village to do a few errands. There are peaches in the refrigerator.

Mother

Clara cut up two peaches and put them in a bowl with some milk. But she was not really hungry, and the peaches did not seem to taste very good. At last she got up and carried her bowl to the sink, letting the water rinse over it slowly, warm against her fingers. Then she went to the living-room doorway and stood looking at the birdcage. The door was still hopefully open, the way

Polly and Teddy had left it, but the cage was empty.

When she went outside, Louise was alone sitting cross-legged in the grass, with her back against a tree trunk. Clara sank down on a lumpy protruding tree root and clasped her hands around her knees. There was a mosquito bite on the back of her wrist and she scratched at it listlessly.

"I was just thinking, maybe squirrel fur would work." Louise was looking up into the branches of the tree.

Clara looked up into the tree too. "A squirrel would be pretty hard to catch."

"Sometimes they get real tame," Louise urged. "Maybe we could get one to come up close if we had some peanuts."

"And hold still while we cut off some fur?"

"Well, maybe."

Clara sighed. The mosquito bite was beginning to bleed and she rubbed at it gently. Here was the human blood. . . .

"Maybe it would." Louise would not give up.

"It says *cat* fur," Clara said darkly. "Nothing else would work."

They sat in silence. Louise pulled up tufts of grass and let the broken silky blades slip through her fingers.

Clara got up and wandered toward the shed, where the dead tree stood and no grass grew. The door was open and Clara stood for a moment in the doorway. She did not even want to go in. The rug hiding the trapdoor lay just as they had left it the morning before. Around it in the dusky gloom everything was just the same—Teddy and Polly's cave, the stack of magazines where she had found the old movie stars' pictures, the oil cans and tools. Near the door a cap and sweater lay on a rickety wooden chair.

Clara recognized the cap and the sweater, which had one pocket torn off and the other sagging out of shape because of the nails and cigarettes and junk that Joe Hooker had stuffed in and out of it over the years. She did not feel much in the mood for fun, but she picked up the sweater and slid her arms into the sleeves.

"*Boo!*"

Louise turned with a whirl, scattering grass blades as Clara jumped around the tree toward her, her hair tucked up under Hooker's cap, the too-long sweater sleeves flapping empty like scarecrow arms.

"Oh, Clara." Louise began to giggle with amusement and relief.

"What're you kids doing with my screens?" Clara pushed back a sleeve and shook a menacing finger at Louise. "I spent all morning painting those screens and you're making a big mess of them."

Louise giggled again.

"And stop that laughing." Clara glowered as fiercely as she could. Louise backed away a step or two, putting her hand to her mouth to hold back the giggling. Clara did look so funny.

"You kids are always ruining my work." Clara advanced with a heavy tread, gesturing angrily.

Louise hid behind a tree and pretended to be scared

of Clara. Her pale thin face peeked around as she tried not to giggle.

"And let me tell you . . . ." Clara lowered her voice threateningly, and Louise ducked back behind the tree. "Let me tell you what happens to kids that tell lies. Bad things—baadd things . . . "

She felt herself being grasped roughly from behind and twisted around by her arm. Then she was staring up at bloodshot eyes and a growth of whiskers that darkened an unshaven face.

"Whadda ya think you're doin'?" Hooker's words were slurred but there was no misunderstanding them.

Clara tried to pull her arm away, but her dark eyes remained fixed with fascination on the ugly whiskery face. Louise looked out from behind the tree, and the muffled giggles died in her throat.

"Whadda ya doin' with my things?"

"I—I thought you didn't want them anymore." Clara tried to pull her arm away, but his grip tightened. "You're hurting my arm!"

Hooker leered at her drunkenly.

"You aren't supposed to come back here anymore." Clara tried to move away, stumbling on a tree root. "Mama told you we didn't need you anymore."

"Whadda *you* know what I'm s'ppose to do." His hand around her arm made Clara wince with pain.

"You're just back here to try to find the witch's treasure," Clara shouted desperately.

Hooker's mouth fell open with surprise, but his grip on Clara's arm did not loosen.

"You are, you are!" Clara felt tears springing to her eyes, Hooker held her arm so tightly.

"Is that so?" His eyes blurred drunkenly.

His face was so close to Clara's that she thought she would faint.

"Well, I'll find it, I'll find it yet," he bragged, his words so slurred now that Clara could hardly understand them. "Nobody thinks old Joe Hooker is worth anything. I'll show them, that's what I'll do. I'll show them all. Joe Hooker's goin' to find that treasure."

"No, you won't." Clara fought to get away, but he held her fast.

"You're hurting my arm."

"Leave my sister alone." Louise tugged at the handyman's arm, but he knocked her away like a pesky fly. Louise fell backward on the grass and sat stunned for a moment, tears rolling down her cheeks.

"Here. Take your old sweater." Clara struggled out of the free sleeve and the sweater dangled around her legs. But Hooker still held her hard by one arm.

"Let me go! Let me go! Take your old sweater." In desperation Clara aimed a kick at Hooker's shin and wrenched her arm loose. The sweater slid off into a heap on the ground.

"Let's get out of here." Clara pulled at Louise who, sniffing back tears, managed to get to her feet. But Hooker blocked their way to the house, and stood, half crouched, with spread arms to catch them if they came past.

"Where d'ya think you're goin' now?" he rasped, enjoying their fright. "Can't get away from the bogey-man."

He lunged at them, and they turned and fled toward the shed, the only place of refuge left. They had a good head start, and Clara slammed the shed door behind them.

"He's coming, he's coming!" There was a dingy dirt-streaked window by the shed door, and by standing on tiptoe Louise could see Hooker weaving unsteadily toward them, his arms still held out wide, as if he might capture the whole shed in his giant grip.

Clara looked around anxiously for something to hold the door. "Here—the toolbox. Help me, Louise."

The toolbox was almost too heavy for them to push, but together they got it with some effort in front of the shed door, just as Joe Hooker began to pound on the outside.

"Hey, you kids, I'll get ya for this—I'll get ya . . ."

Clara yanked the rug away from the trapdoor. "Hurry up! Down here," she ordered Louise.

Louise did not hesitate. Already she could see the tool box moving a few inches as the door banged against it. She went down the ladder as fast as she could, and Clara was so close behind that she stepped on Louise's fingers.

Utter darkness enveloped the room below as the trap-door closed. Balancing on the ladder, Clara fumbled to find the bolt on the underside of the door. It was stuck, and she struggled with it desperately until at last with a raggedy screechy sound it loosened, slid across, and locked.

They stood blindly in the darkness, hearts pounding. Above them at the shed door the sounds of banging continued along with muffled angry oaths. Then there was silence.

"He's gone." Clara's eyes hunted for Louise in the darkness, but she could see nothing. She felt along the tabletop until her fingers came to the box of kitchen matches they had left there, and the candle they had used the morning before. Her hands were trembling, and at first she didn't think she could strike the match.

The flicker of flame caught on the candlewick and threw wavering light on the pale, frightened face of Louise, who stood crouched back against the wall.

Just then above them they heard the noise at the shed door again and the unmistakable sound of the toolbox grating on the floor. Joe Hooker was forcing it out of the way with the door.

Then they heard his steps on the shed floor and the sound of things being shoved around. Something made of glass fell and broke with a heavy crash.

"I'll get you kids. Think you can make fun of me . . ."

They heard him stumble and fall, and there was silence again for a moment. Clara held her breath. Maybe he had knocked himself unconscious. But no, after a moment they heard his steps again, right over their heads now, and then they heard him tugging at the trapdoor. Clara looked up fearfully. She didn't think the bolt was very strong, or that it was very likely to hold if someone really pulled hard—and Joe Hooker was strong, even as drunk as he was. The bolt was old and rusty. Already

Clara could hear the sound of the screws tearing in the wood.

"Oh-h—do something," Louise wailed from her corner.

Clara's heart was pounding faster than ever, and her mouth was so dry she couldn't swallow. Frantically she looked around for something to defend them if Hooker came down the ladder, but there didn't seem to be anything handy to use as a weapon.

Almost before she realized what she was doing, Clara found herself standing in the witch's circle beside the crumbly heap of mandrake root and pure earth. She tugged the cap from her head and her dark hair swirled down around her shoulders.

Louise was too frightened even to speak, as Clara tossed Hooker's cap down upon the magic mixture. "By the seven powers of the seven powers of darkness, I will make you disappear," Clara began the incantation in a breathless rush. She could not get the words out fast enough. "Mandrake root and pure earth; I will make you disappear."

The only thing she could see in the candlelight was the startled face of Louise as she pressed closer back against the shelves holding the jars of bats' blood and eyes of toads.

"All that is known to the darkness and the seven powers of the seven darknesses. . . . " Clara raced on as the bolt above screeched loose. " . . . take you, take you, take you."

CHAPTER ELEVEN

Everything was silent in the shed above. The rattling of the trapdoor had stopped. Louise and Clara hardly dared to breathe.

"Has he gone away?"

Clara held a finger to her lips. Her ears strained for the sound of retreating footsteps or of the shed door closing. But no sound came.

After what seemed like a long, long time, Clara went up the ladder. Its worn rungs creaked in the stillness. She listened again, her face pressed close to the trapdoor. What if it was only a trick and Joe Hooker was crouched there on the other side of the door, waiting silently and motionlessly, so they would think they were safe, and come out?

At last Clara opened the door a few inches. A thin line of light fell across her face. As Louise watched from below, Clara lifted the door a few more inches, and then a few more.

"It's all right," Clara whispered down. "He's gone away."

"Are you sure? Maybe he's hiding behind something." Louise did not budge from her place against the wall.

"I don't see him anywhere."

But still Louise waited while Clara went up into the shed. She could hear Clara walking around.

Then Clara's head appeared at the trapdoor. "He's not here. Put out the candle and come up."

Louise blew out the candle and went up the ladder warily. She stuck her head out and looked around. Clara was right. Hooker was gone. The shed door hung ajar, and the rug had been thrown halfway across the floor.

Louise came out slowly, looking over her shoulders at the corners of the shed, but there was an emptiness about the place and a feeling that they were alone there now. Joe Hooker was really gone.

Louise looked at Clara with an unspoken question, and Clara said rather brusquely, "He just got tired of chasing us and went away."

"He didn't take his car," Louise said. Through the open shed door she could see Joe Hooker's battered Ford parked between the house and the roadway.

The girls stood close together at the shed door and looked across the shaded yard. There was a queer, abandoned look about the paint-rusted old car as it stood under the trees.

"Why didn't he take his car?" Louise asked in a hushed voice.

"He must still be somewhere around," Clara answered uneasily.

But although they stood there a long time, watching and listening for some sign, there was nothing, only an ominous silence that lay heavily over the yard and house.

"Mama's home," Louise cried with a note of relief as Mrs. Astin's car pulled into the driveway behind Joe Hooker's car.

They waited a moment longer, still rather afraid to venture from the shed.

"Well, let's go," Clara said at last. "If he's still around, Mama will make him leave."

They began to cross the yard, and Polly dashed to greet them.

"Mama bought me some red shoes!"

"Is that man here again?" Mrs. Astin was saying, more to herself than to anyone else. She was taking packages from the back seat of the car, and she didn't wait for anyone to answer her. "Clara, Louise, help me with these things. Teddy, be careful, dear, I think that bag has the eggs in it." Mrs. Astin shook her head as she closed the car door.

Everyone had packages to carry into the house, and Polly and Teddy raced ahead, thumping up the porch steps.

Mrs. Astin frowned and shook her head again as she walked past Joe Hooker's Ford. Her glance skimmed over the yard. "Now where is he? I wonder. I told him there was nothing more to fix."

Louise looked at Clara, appealing for directions, but Clara kept her eyes down and wouldn't look back at Louise as they followed their mother through the house to the kitchen.

"You girls can start putting the groceries away," Mrs. Astin murmured absently. "I'm going to step out to the shed a minute and speak with Mr. Hooker."

Louise felt that she might start to cry again, but still Clara would not look at her.

It was not many minutes before Mrs. Astin returned.

"If that doesn't beat all," she said with exasperation. "He's gone off somewhere and left that old car filling up half the driveway. Honestly!"

Polly patted her mother's arm. "He'll be back soon."

Clara and Louise were not so sure.

CHAPTER TWELVE

Joe Hooker's car stood in the driveway for two days. At night Clara and Louise could see it from their bedroom window, a looming shadow under the trees, the windshield glimmering in the moonlight. It was like a ghost car, Louise thought.

On the third day, Monday morning, a police car drove out from town, and the children stood clustered like weeds about the porch steps and listened while their mother talked to the policeman.

"It's not unusual for Hooker to take off for a few days," the policeman said to Mrs. Astin. He took off his hat and eased the crease it had made on his forehead. His voice lowered, although the children could catch a word now and then. "Hooker drinks quite a bit and sometimes goes off on a binge."

"Yes, I had heard that he drank some," Mrs. Astin

said, with a sideways glance toward the children. "I suspected he had been drinking a few times when he was here. I told him not to come again. I can't imagine why he would come here and then go away and leave his car."

The officer shrugged. "When people get to drinking . . . " He left the sentence for Mrs. Astin to finish for herself.

She nodded wisely. "They aren't responsible for their actions," she agreed. "But after all this time, I did feel I should call you."

"Well, he lives with his sister in town. He'll turn up there before long, I expect." The policeman smoothed his hair and put his hat on again. "In the meantime, I'll tell her the car's here."

Before he left, the policeman looked inside the car—the children wondered for what. A clue to where Mr. Hooker was?

Then the squad car drove away, and Mrs. Astin stood watching after it with a despondent feeling. A fine summer place they had for themselves. A drunken handyman leaving work undone and a rusting old jalopy in the driveway.

Later that day Joe Hooker's sister walked out from town and drove the car away. Everyone felt relieved that it was gone, though at first Teddy could imagine that Joe Hooker still lurked somewhere, crouched behind a tree ready to spring out at him—*the bogeyman will get you* —while Polly, cuddling in Clara's lap that night, murmured sleepily, "I don't like this house. It's spooky."

But as the rest of the week passed, Polly and Teddy

forgot about Joe Hooker. They ran around barefooted and ate peanut butter sandwiches in the yard and banged at the old croquet balls. They dragged a lot of stuff into the shed for their cave, and tried to remember to wear their good-luck charms. They had learned that if they forgot, either Clara or Louise was sure to remind them. Although the canary cage remained empty, the twins never gave up hope that their "birdie" would come back, and every day they asked their mother when Daddy was coming.

"Saturday," she always said. Mrs. Astin spoke calmly and cheerfully, but in the back of her mind she was already thinking: Saturday. And I hope by Sunday we'll be gone. She hadn't told the children yet, but she had made up her mind that she could not spend the rest of the summer in this dismal house, and she intended to tell Mr. Astin so.

For Clara and Louise the days passed with increasing uneasiness. Even afternoons at the swimming pool and dinner one evening at the Village Inn didn't help.

In the dim old-fashioned room at the Village Inn the bear head loomed ominously in half-shadow, and Louise watched wistfully through the windows at the gathering dusk. She almost wished she would see Mr. Hooker walking by on the street. Wouldn't that solve everything?

But she didn't see him.

Nor as time passed were there any reports that Joe Hooker had returned to his sister's house, and although Clara and Louise thumbed ceaselessly through the pages of *The Book of Witches,* they discovered nothing that was helpful except the ritual for "Appearances" that they had already found. And they had no cat!

The weather remained muggy and the sky overcast.

"Why don't you two get outside more?" Mrs. Astin said to the two girls one afternoon. "I don't see why you want to spend so much time upstairs."

But Mrs. Astin's mind was on other things, and she did not worry long about Clara and Louise.

Louise sat in the rocking chair and it creaked back and forth, the only sound in the room. She was tired of looking through the book. They wouldn't find anything. She wanted to go home and sleep in her own bed again.

But Clara couldn't give up. If Mr. Hooker never came back, the lady in the bookshop would remember that Clara had bought a book about witchcraft—and that their house was the last place where Mr. Hooker had been seen. The finger of guilt would point straight at Clara. She *had* to find something, and so the soft sound of the pages turning in *The Book of Witches* joined the creak, creak, creak of Louise's rocking chair.

In fire is my power, in numbers is my power. . . . Clara leafed on through the book.

Mandrake root and pure earth; I will make you disappear. . . .

Clara wished she had never seen *that* page.

Destruction of Witches:

The only way to destroy a witch was to burn her. In one instance a witch was stoned to death in a village, her body buried in a field. But it was said that at night this corpse roamed the streets; children wailed with sickness, crops failed, streams dried up. At last the crude coffin was dug up again and the shriveled remains within were burned.

In another instance, a witch had been burned at the stake, but ill fortune still stalked the town until one day a crumbling hut was discovered in a nearby woods. This had been the witch's secret haunt, and only when it too had been burned to the ground was the full evil of the witch destroyed.

Clara's dark eyes grew thoughtful. The words of the woman at the bookshop echoed in her memory. *Nobody ever seems to want to stay there very long. . . . People here in town say it's haunted, that it still has a spell over it . . .*

Maybe if the shed were burned. Clara thought . . .

If the shed were burned, the last remaining evil of the witch would be destroyed. People could live in the little house happily.

Clara felt as though perhaps she had found the answer, but the feeling slid away illusively, as fast as it had come. Whom could she tell? Grown-ups would laugh and say it was all superstitious nonsense from ancient days. Surely she couldn't take it upon herself to burn down the shed.

Clara closed the book and stared at the cover. Somehow it did not look quite the same. Her fingers traced the raised scrolled letters of the title. Had they been raised so high before? Had the cover been so soft, so dark? Now it was almost black, and the book felt larger and heavier in her hands. It was as though the book were changing, growing. Soon the scrolled letters would rise up as if from a black swampy mire, while the pages within grew larger, the pictures bigger. Perhaps they would come to life, and the spiders and snakes and bats would seep out through the soft mire of the binding . . . be there in the room with her. . . .

Louise twisted a lock of hair and creaked back and forth in the rocking chair. Her eyelids drooped sadly, and the room grew dimmer as the afternoon wore on.

On Thursday morning the girls' spirits sank to an even lower point when they overheard their mother on the telephone. She was talking to their father.

"When you get here Saturday, you'll see what I mean. It's such a cheerless sort of house. I know you'll agree I just can't take it for the whole summer."

Louise and Clara exchanged startled looks. What did that mean? How soon were they going to leave?

Their questions were soon answered. Mrs. Astin replaced the receiver and turned to them with a wry smile. "Well, chickies, I hope you won't be too disappointed, but I think we will be leaving when Daddy comes."

Louise looked at Clara.

"When Daddy comes?" Clara tried to sound calm. "Aren't we going to stay all summer?"

"Not *here,* " Mrs. Astin said.

"But"—Clara searched for words—"but what about all the money we paid for it?"

"I don't know about that." Mrs. Astin waved a hand

vaguely. "But it will all work out. There's nothing for you two to worry about." She paused a moment and then added, "I just hope the twins won't be too disappointed. They've been having such a good time in that shed."

Her gaze drifted fondly to the kitchen window, where she could just see a bit of the shed far back in the yard beyond the trees.

"Well," she said at last, "we've got a good part of the summer left; we'll find someplace nice to go. Maybe a cottage by a beach somewhere." She began to run water at the sink and hardly noticed when Clara and Louise went silently back upstairs to their room.

They were frantic now. Time was running out. Daddy was coming Saturday, and then they would have to leave.

"Oh, Clara, what will we do?" Louise's eyes were large in her pale, thin face. "What will we *do?* "

"Be quiet and let me think," Clara said. Her mind was going a hundred miles a minute, but no answers came.

"Oh, if only we had some cat fur." Clara clenched her fists, her dark eyes burning.

"But we don't," Louise wailed fretfully. "We don't."

Then finally, late that afternoon a stray cat strolled through the trees onto the front lawn. Gaunt and thin, it stood amid the tilted croquet wickets and stared at the house with an unwavering, unfathomable gaze.

CHAPTER THIRTEEN

The witch's room had never seemed so eerie to Louise. The shadows in the corners had never seemed so deep. She kept looking around into the gloom, expecting she knew not what to step out of it into the candlelight.

"What's the matter with you?" Clara challenged nervously.

"I just want to get it done and get out of here."

"I'm not afraid." Clara looked about her defiantly and tossed her dark hair back from her face. "Here, hold this."

Louise took Joe Hooker's cap with just the tips of her fingers and watched as Clara cleared away the mandrake root and pure earth, pricked her finger with a needle, and squeezed a few drops of blood down upon the tufts of cat fur she had put inside the magic circle. Human blood and fur of cat . . .

"Give me the hat."

Louise handed the cap over mutely, and then she put her hand behind her back and crossed two fingers for luck. If the disappearing spell had worked, the appearing spell should work too, but she was crossing her fingers for extra-good measure.

Clara began to say the words, and the dark pressed close against Louise. "From the unknown, from the far-away places of the darkness, I summon you. Come through fire and earthquake and darkness. I summon you."

They went up and looked around. There was no sight of Joe Hooker in the shed or yard.

"Maybe things don't come back to the same place they disappeared from," Louise ventured, as they stood looking at the deserted grounds. "Maybe Mr. Hooker appeared back at his sister's house—or somewhere in town—or some other place."

Clara considered this. It was an unfortunate development, if true. If Mr. Hooker was going to appear at some random spot—why, the world was a big place! They might never know whether he had appeared at all, whether their spell had worked or not, particularly if they had to go away themselves when Daddy came.

"I know," Clara said suddenly. "Let's try to make the canary appear again and see what happens. It's small, it ought to be easy to get back, easier than a great big person. If it appears back in the cage, we'll at least know that much."

"But if it's not in the cage, we still won't know whether it appeared somewhere else, or whether the spell just doesn't work." Louise looked at Clara dejectedly. She did not want to go back down into that witch's room. Ever.

"It's worth a try," Clara insisted. "We can't stop now, can we?"

They made their way once more down the ladder into the dank room below the shed. Clara lighted the candle again.

"Find those canary feathers; they've got to be here somewhere."

Louise poked a foot gingerly at the mandrake root and pure earth. One feather clung, dingy with dirt. Louise closed her eyes and picked it out. The other feather they could not find.

"One will do," Clara said with determination.

And she began again; "From the unknown, from the faraway places of the darkness, I summon you. Come through fire and earthquake and darkness. I summon you."

They waited a few moments, the words a whispery echo around them.

"Come on," Clara said finally, "Let's go see." She went first up the ladder, talking to Louise over her shoulder. "Won't Mama be pleased if the canary came back?"

Mrs. Astin was far from pleased. On the contrary, she was more upset by the sudden reappearance of the canary in a cage that had stood empty for so many days than she had been by its disappearance. She stood gawking at the flutter of yellow wings. The canary's disappearance could somehow be explained by a cage door left carelessly open, even though no one admitted to having done so. Its reappearance, alive, cocky, and bright-eyed, could have no explanation at all that she could understand.

"How could that *be?*" she said dumbfoundedly to Polly, the only one present.

Polly heard Clara and Louise coming and ran out to the kitchen to meet them.

"Our birdie's back," she shrieked with joy "It flew in a window when we weren't looking and went right back into its cage to get its seed. Come and see." She raced back to the living room.

Clara and Louise edged as far as the living-room doorway. Polly was undoubtedly happy, they could see that. She hopped about the cage clapping her hands.

But their mother gave them a distracted look and threw up her hands in defeat. "This is the last straw. Absolutely the last straw. I don't know if I will even wait for your father to come Saturday. I might just go upstairs and pack my clothes this very *minute.*"

She hurried by them, pale and excited, and they could hear her steps as she went upstairs, muttering to herself.

"Hello, birdie," Polly was chirping happily.

Clara and Louise looked after their mother's retreating figure. She was going to pack *now,* and they still didn't have Mr. Hooker back.

By suppertime, however, it appeared that Mrs. Astin had decided not to pack up right away, after all. She had decided to wait until Mr. Astin came, but it was difficult for her. She went about the kitchen with a long-suffering calmness and did not hear the children when they spoke to her. After supper she went upstairs to her room to have a nap, if she could sleep with all the things that plagued her mind. She lay down wearily and wished it were Saturday.

Polly and Teddy had jiggled all the dials they could get hold of on the old television set until they had one channel coming in well enough for them to watch it, and they lay on their stomachs on the living-room floor enjoying a Western. The canary dipped its yellow head up and down at the seed cup.

"We can hold out for another two days," said a man at a fort. A woman sobbed and dabbed at her eyes with a pioneer apron. Rattles of gunfire sounded.

Clara and Louise sat on the back-porch steps. An early twilight invaded the tree-locked yard, coming in like mist through the close branches and the prickle of leaves outlined against the sky.

"At least we know the canary came back in the same place," Clara said. Her eyes narrowed speculatively. "Daddy will be here Saturday, and then we'll probably go away. We've got to try again tonight."

"Tonight?" Louise gaped at Clara. Louise wasn't going down into that witch's room at *night*.

"Can't we try tomorrow?"

Clara shook her head firmly. "What if Mama changes her mind again? What if in the morning she says, 'We're going now'?"

Louise thought about that, gripping her knees closer. She felt cold and shivery in the warm summer evening.

"It's got to be tonight." Clara stood up boldly. "I'll get the flashlight."

Twilight had crept into the house, and only the pale-blue light from the television set glowed in the living room. There was no other light on in the house as Clara groped in the kitchen drawer. Indian war whoops came to her faintly from across the hall.

Outside again, Clara went down the back-porch steps and started across the yard. Louise followed her with a sinking heart.

The shed was silent in the darkening night. Teddy and Polly's cave with its trappings and furnishings occupied nearly half the floor by now. The tool chest they had pushed in front of the door to stop Joe Hooker was still near the door, a solid reminder of that frantic morning.

The trapdoor creaked on its hinges; the room below lay in blackness. Clara lighted the candle again and placed it beside *The Book of Witches*, which lay on the table opened to the page with the incantation for "*Appearances.*" Louise stood back by the flimy curtain with its black stars and dark moon.

But once again, after Clara had carefully said the magic words, the shed above remained deserted.

"Let's go," Louise pleaded. "It isn't going to work."

"Maybe you should try." Clara did not like to admit

that she could not work the magic, but she was willing to try anything.

"*Me?*" Louise backed farther away from the magic circle.

"And let's light more candles, too. *In fire is my power.*" Clara rummaged along the dusty shelves. "Here's one . . . and here's one . . . . "

"I don't want to," Louise begged, watching with a mounting sense of doom as Clara found more candles and lighted them one by one.

In all, six candles lined the table now. The room brightened. The shadows retreated deeper into the corners, like wolves slinking away from a campfire light.

Clara cocked her head upward once more, but all was silent in the shed above.

"Get in the circle," she directed Louise, but Louise only remained cowering against the tapestry, her shoulders hunched, her eyes closed tightly. Clara pulled her into the circle, but even then Louise would not open her eyes. She thought she might faint and fall to the ground if she looked at the cat fur and the human blood. Clara had to prompt her with the words, and Louise's voice, repeating after Clara, trembled out into the candlelight barely above a whisper.

They stood and waited, but no sound came from anywhere in the night.

"I'll go and look," Clara said in a low voice.

She went up the ladder, while Louise stood frozen in the circle.

There was no one in the shed. Clara tiptoed to the door

103

and gazed into the yard, but she saw only the full dark of night and the gaunt outlines of the trees. No Joe Hooker.

"Oh, Clara, what will we do?" Louise opened her eyes at last, close to tears. It seemed a wicked thing they had done, and now they could not undo it. Mr. Hooker would stay disappeared forever.

Clara sat disconsolately on the bottom rung of the ladder, and Louise came to huddle beside her. "I guess we'll have to keep trying as long as we can," Clara said at last.

Then they heard footsteps running across the shed floor above, and Teddy's face appeared at the open trapdoor. Polly was close beside him, and they stared down into the brightness of the candles.

In fire is my power, in numbers is my power. . . . Clara looked up at the two small faces shining in the candlelight. *In fire is my power, in numbers is my power.* The words appeared clearly in Clara's mind—she had read over those pages so many times.

Before Louise realized what she was doing, Clara had pushed her aside from the ladder and was calling up to the twins, "Come down here, right away!"

"There's mice," Polly protested.

Clara was growing more and more excited. "Don't you see, Louise? In fire and in *numbers.* There's two of them, twins—they're special." She turned back to look up at the open trapdoor again. "Come down, right away!"

"There's mice," Polly repeated, puckering up her small rosy mouth.

"No, there aren't," Clara said wildly, scrambling toward her up the ladder. "Come down, we need your help." She seized Polly's arm as Louise stared up at the struggle.

"Now come down." Clara was tugging at Polly. "Louise and I are here. There's nothing to be afraid of."

"I'm not afraid," Teddy declared. "I like this place."

Polly, being careful of her new red shoes, came down slowly with her pudgy fingers tight on the ladder rungs. Her hair hung in her eyes, and her ears were pricked for the sounds of mice.

"We don't have much time," Clara explained rapidly. How long would their mother's nap continue? What if she came out to the shed looking for them? "You two stand right here." She drew Polly and Teddy into the witch's circle beside Joe Hooker's cap and the wad of cat's fur sticky with blood.

Every candle burned—every candle they had been able to find. Clara's glance swept the room one last time. *In fire is my power, in numbers is my power, in the circle is my power.* Was there anything else she could do?

"Here, take these." She gave each twin a candle to hold and waited one second more, but no further inspiration came to her.

"Now together you repeat what I say," she commanded the twins.

"I want to go home." Polly's candle wobbled and shadows quivered on her face.

"It will only take a minute." Clara changed her tactics and became soothing, although it was hard to be calm.

She stroked Polly's hair and smiled reassuringly. "Say what I say, and then we'll go see if there's some ice cream left. Okay?"

Polly hung her head sadly.

"Now," Clara said again, keeping her voice as soft and soothing as she could, "together you two say what I say, both of you, as if you were reciting a poem together."

Louise gripped her thin fingers on the lower ladder rungs and waited.

CHAPTER FOURTEEN

"From the unknown, from the faraway places of the darkness," Clara began urgently.

Polly looked up over her candle with one last silent appeal to be allowed to go.

"*Please.*" Clara's face floated in the candlelight, streaked with darkness. Her eyes, encircled with shadow, were tremendous. "From the unknown, from the faraway places of the darkness . . . "

"From the unknown, from the faraway places of the darkness." The twins' voices faltered and faded. They stared at Clara as if hypnotized.

"I summon you," Clara prompted.

"I summon you."

"Come through fire and earthquake and darkness."

"I want to go home," Polly begged.

Clara shook her dark head frantically. "Come through fire and earthquake and darkness—go *on*, Polly."

Polly's faint voice joined Teddy's. "Come through fire and earthquake and darkness."

"I summon you."

"I summon you."

Louise did not dare breathe, as the unsteady little voices faded away to stillness and the last words of the incantation were done. . . . And then, above them, they heard the sound of boxes being shoved around and Joe Hooker's rough voice. "I'll get you, you little brats. Make fun of me, will you?"

The trapdoor flew open with a furious yank. Joe Hooker stared down at them with bloodshot eyes, his face distorted and grotesque in the glowing light from the room below.

Louise screamed and dodged away as the drunken man lunged down the ladder toward her, and Clara felt a hard thump against her side as Polly dropped her candle and flung herself at her.

"Go away! Go away!!" Clara cried out to Hooker, backing into a corner with Polly clinging and stumbling beside her.

"Go away! Go away!" Teddy shouted. Hooker reached the foot of the ladder and swung out at Teddy who crouched under the table screaming.

"Run, Teddy, run!" Clara cried, holding her arms protectively around Polly. They were as far back in the corner as they could go, and as she called out, Hooker swung around and lurched toward her. He looked towering in the wavering shadows, and with a raging swing he knocked bottles from the shelves, sending a rain of jars down upon the earth floor. There they rolled and jarred together, into the magic circle, under the table, over the heap of cat fur and human blood.

Louise dragged Teddy out from under the table and bolted for the ladder, while the bottles fell and smashed and rolled.

"*Help!*" Clara shrieked, but Hooker caught her and pulled her from the corner. Polly clung to her legs as the jars tumbled about under their feet.

"Clara," Louise called in panic from the top of the ladder.

Clara fought to break away from Hooker's grasp. The table gave way and turned over as Hooker backed into it with the struggling Clara. She bent her head and bit hard into his arm above the wrist.

"Damn brat!" He jerked away, stumbling against the shelves and sending the last few jars crashing down.

Clara pushed Polly ahead of her up the ladder and kicked back with an anguished cry as she felt Hooker's hand close upon her ankle. The kick hit Hooker across the cheek, and he reeled back with pain. His grip loosened, and Clara scrambled free, falling upward upon the shed floor with dark hair flying.

"*Run, run!*" Louise pulled at Clara as Polly and Teddy excaped away into the darkened yard beyond.

"I'll get you," the voice roared from below. Hooker came up the ladder. Clara and Louise dashed out of the shed door, panting and terrified.

"Mama, Mama!" Teddy screamed, racing toward the house with Polly close behind.

Joe Hooker swayed drunkenly in the shed doorway, and as Clara threw one last terrified look back, she saw him begin to stagger across the yard toward the woods, holding on to the tree trunks for support.

A light went on in an upstairs bedroom, and Mrs. Astin's face appeared at the window. She stared down, still dazed with sleep, as the four children streaked across the dark yard and thundered up the porch steps like a stampede of wild animals with all the demons in the world in pursuit.

Behind the fleeing children, candles from the upset table ignited the tattered curtain hanging in the witch's room, and in the silence a steady fire began, which soon reached through the shed floor and ignited an overturned can of gasoline.

The shed burned rapidly after that, there was no saving it. The carpet that had concealed the trapdoor smoldered and blazed; flames spread through the cave Teddy and Polly had so carefully made, leaped at the ancient, dry wood of the window frames, and cast an eerie light across the dark yard.

Fire engines sped out from town under the distressed screech of sirens, but the firemen could do nothing except wet down the charred and gaping walls of the shed and prevent the fire from spreading to the house.

The shelves that had contained the jars of bats' blood and dove hearts and deadly nightshade burned and fell, and *The Book of Witches,* fallen open on the floor, curled up at the corners of the pages as the flames licked at it, illuminating the words in one last ghastly glow before they were consumed to ashes . . . *mandrake root and pure earth . . . I will make you disappear. . . .*